Lincolnshire
COUNTY COUNCIL

COMMUNITIES, CULTURAL SERVICES and ADULT EDUCATION

This book should be returned on or before the last date shown below. SA1

To renew or order library books please telephone 01522 782010
or visit www.lincolnshire.gov.uk

You will require a Personal Identification Number.
Ask any member of staff for this.

Bodyswap

The Boy who was 84

L. P. Howarth

CATNIP BOOKS
Published by Catnip Publishing Ltd.
14 Greville Street
London EC1N 8SB

This edition published 2009
1 3 5 7 9 10 8 6 4 2

A CIP catalogue record for this book is available from the British Library

ISBN: 978-1-84647-075-2

Printed in Poland

www.catnippublishing.co.uk

Contents

The Name's Hornbeam

Will Dudgeon raised a dripping bunch of irises from his bucket and considered the silver vase. Flower arranging hadn't been *exactly* what he'd had in mind as a Saturday job at the Lisle Island Hotel, but he guessed it came with the territory.

'You done reception yet?' called housekeeper Mrs Rhymer.

'Jus' about.'

'Get a wriggle on, there's the dining-room troughs, and the bar, and a party checking in at eleven!'

Six vases to fill – she'd notice if he skimped, or stuffed them full of foliage – plus a special one on the desk, and two at the bottom of the stairs. Will looked around, annoyed about having to refresh his buckets from the mess of blooms in the pantry two or three times, at least.

Beyond the annoying empty vases, the usual view across to the mainland stretched beyond the foyer doors. His home at the only pub on the island, the Pilchard Inn, showed its red roof beyond the golf course. Last summer Will had made a nice little earner out of picking golf balls out of the gorse; this autumn, management had insisted that the only job available was Flower Boy.

He'd kept it a secret at school, and from his mates, of course. Yo, Wilma, they'd say. Going up Saturday morning cinema? Nah, he'd say carelessly. Gotta help the old man out, haven't I?

He never went into details and so they all assumed he helped at the pub, which he did, but the money was better at the stylish Lisle Island Hotel, which dreamed it still existed in the nineteen twenties, when an eccentric millionaire had built it. This was its main appeal, so customers expected posh flower displays in its extravagant troughs and vases. Mrs Rhymer had repeatedly shown Will how to do them, but he never spent more'n three minutes on any of 'em else the title 'Flower Boy' might get to him, and there were a whole heap of other jobs to do …

Now the first of the silver vases waited in reception. Water streaming up his sleeves as usual, Will crammed the flowers down its neck and moved them around a bit. They squeaked as he tried to arrange them. He should take some out probably, and arrange some ferns to set them off. The purple blooms with their open yellow throats looked a bit bald with only their own foliage. He could shove in a lily or two. But then there were all the other displays to be done, and how much time was he spending on them, anyway, not to mention the watering …

'*You look like a strong young man.*'

The voice whispered close to his ear. Will jumped out of his skin.

'No need to jump like a startled antelope – I don't bite, you know!' The oldest man Will had ever seen in his life stood at his elbow. There was something a little repulsive about the way he was so extremely close, so that Will could feel the breath from his laugh, like a draught from a rotten door.

He couldn't help it. Will recoiled. 'Didn't get you, did I?'

'I remain unsplashed with water, if that's what you mean.' Another fetid bark – the oldest laugh, from the throat of the oldest man in creation. His withered lips drew away from grey gums. He dislodged his false teeth and stuck out the upper set grotesquely, and winked. 'Can't do that, can you? Advantages of age.'

There weren't many other advantages that Will could see. 'Housekeeper's in the kitchen,' he offered politely.

'It was you I came to see.'

The intense stare of the old man's red eyes was getting to him now. It occurred to Will that he might have been watching the jamming of the irises into the vase. 'I don't usually force 'em in – the flowers, I mean – but we're pushed for time this morning.'

'Pushed, are you?' The stranger gave it an unpleasant

emphasis. 'Too busy to spare an old man a moment? Name's Hornbeam.' He extended a claw, and Will had to shake it. 'Strapping lad like you. Arranging flowers.'

'That's just part of the job, there's watering and bins and—'

'Must be a chore, doing all these displays on your own when no doubt you'd rather be climbing trees.'

'Takes for ever,' Will admitted. At least someone noticed how much he did. But the old man was creeping him out. 'Better get on and finish.'

He took up his buckets and crossed the black-and-white tiles to enter the dining room with its lonely piano and graceful, shrouded tables. Bending to start filling the flower troughs, he realized that the old man had followed him.

'You're gold, you are,' the suggestive voice creaked at his elbow. 'Strapping lad like you. Responsible as well – not something you find often these days.'

This Mister Hornbeam's eyes were boring into his mind and loosening his tongue. Before he knew what he was doing, Will was complaining about his job to a perfect stranger: 'Stupid tiled floors, if you drop any water on 'em you have to go and get the mop, else people slip up an' sue you.' He chocked a trough with gladioli, adding some big, wavy blooms that no one with a life knew the name of. 'Plus the ballroom's a nightmare to polish with some old machine that looks like an upside-down pelican—'

'Sometimes old is best, like good wine.' The red eyes saw his annoyance. A chill ran up Will's back. He couldn't move or think. Then somehow the old man released him, and laughed. 'But, of course, you're right. Who wouldn't rather be young, and strong?'

Will filled two troughs and hurried to finish a third. He dived into the kitchen and found that Mrs Rhymer had set out two more buckets filled with pink and white blooms. He dragged them back to the dining room and found the old man pouring icy cascades of notes from the piano and pounding its lower registers like thunder. He stopped abruptly. 'I once had a talented body – a talent for music, I mean.'

'Better leave the piano alone or Mrs Rhymer'll have you,' Will warned. 'Unless you're a guest, I mean.'

'A guest – hah! Why not?' The old man watched Will finish the last vase by the door.

What did he care whether the old codger checked in or not? Will hurried to be done with it. As he was introducing the last, endy bits of some pink spray or other to an elegant tub of lilies, Mister Hornbeam touched some thrilling keys and began to play again.

Will knew he should refresh the slim vases on top of the piano with something elegant. Instead he rattled his buckets around and pointedly swept some stems towards the door. 'That'll be it then.'

More thrilling descents from high notes, and intricate figures.

'Ah-hem!' Will secured one of the dining-room doors. 'This room's usu'lly closed up till lunch.'

The music stopped as if it had been choked. The piano lid came down with a clipped sound. He didn't hear the old man cross the floor. In the space of time it took Will to reach up and secure the second French door with a bolt, the voice was at his elbow. '*When were you last ill?*'

The red eyes were gripping his mind again, and he could do nothing but try to answer: 'Throwing-up bug at Easter?'

'Nothing serious then.'

'Everybody had it. Neil Tamblyn threw up in maths.' Will felt sick, remembering.

'And you've had the usual chickenpox and measles …?'

'Mum didn't like the jabs,' Will said humbly. 'I just do odd jobs here on Saturdays, I'm not anyone important and I'd like to go now. So – if you don't mind –' His voice sounded strange in his ears. '– I've got to get on.'

• ● •

Mister W.D. Hornbeam – for that was his name – raised a sunset-coloured toast to Will Dudgeon's health precisely thirteen minutes later. 'You'll show an old man around. Why not start with the bar?'

'The domed glass ceiling dates from nineteen twenty-two,' Will read faintly from the *Guide to Lisle*

Island Hotel. 'The mirrored bar and pool with goldfish were installed by millionaire Archie Trice to amuse his guests.'

'A toast.'

Will found a glass in his hand. 'What's in it?'

'A taste to surpass all you've ever tasted before. Your health!'

The last few minutes had been a blank. No sign of his buckets or flowers. Will wondered where Mike, the barman, was. Behind him the fountain plinked over the goldfish and beyond the balmy conservatory the hotel seemed to slumber. W.D. Hornbeam winked. Will was left with the clear impression he'd been trying to guess Hornbeam's name. 'William?'

'Same as yours,' Hornbeam replied. 'Drink up.'

'Then Darren or Dennis?' Will stalled.

'Darren. At my age. Ha-ha,' his ancient host guffawed. 'Deforest,' said Hornbeam, sobering. 'Actually William Deforest.'

'Strange name.'

'Strange man who gave it to me. Actually William Deforest James.'

'How many names have you got?'

The lips shrank back in a smile: 'If I listed all of them they'd stretch back through five thousand years. But I won't need to change it this time, as I'm a William already, *conveniently*.'

Hornbeam's red eye watched him, magnified

maniacally through his cocktail. Not for the first time, Will felt compelled to raise his glass.

'Cheers!'

The fiery-looking cocktail had crept to very brink of his glass, within a whisper of Will's waiting lips – 'Wait!' – before Hornbeam had nimbly crossed the bar with a horrible quick agility, like a frog after a fly, to dunk a cocktail umbrella into his glass.

'Your health!' Hornbeam threw back his head so that the tendons in his stringy neck stood out like organ pipes.

It seemed rude to miss the moment. In the instant before he swallowed, it seemed to Will that his cocktail changed colour – that a flush of pink powder had blossomed under the cocktail umbrella. Too late now. The fragrant liquid had slid down like Chinese silk before he could question or check it.

And after all, nothing had changed. Archie Trice's goldfish – or goldfish very like them – still swam in their pool unconcernedly like slivers of gold in a South Seas reef. He was the same Will, sitting on the same stool he'd sat on other Saturdays to jaw with Mike, or watch footie in Mike's back room, before knocking off at two and going home. Admittedly his knees felt like someone else's, and the angle at which they rested against his bar stool looked strange. So his elbows felt like furniture and his tongue like a cushion. He was just the same. The same Will Dudgeon, on just the same stool – wasn't he?

· ● ·

'Archie Trice,' Hornbeam reflected. 'A millionaire at fourteen. Now *there's* a body worth stealing.'

'A what?'

'A jolly good feeling,' said Hornbeam. 'Goes down like a rocket, doesn't it?'

Will had to admit that it did. The photos lining the walls swam in front of his eyes, and the light came in through Archie's glass roof like a rain of diamonds. In a careless way he got up and examined the silver-framed history of the millionaire's life: Archie Trice playing tennis with flappers, or lounging against his silver Bentley, Archie Trice in a striped bathing suit, Archie Trice singing in front of a band, Trice playing golf, Trice laughing with friends who looked like middle-aged people in fancy dress. He looked middle-aged himself, Will thought, catching his reflection in a frame of Archie playing croquet. He, Will, could imagine what he'd look like in old age. His chin would double, his cheeks would sag. First they'd grow fat and slumpy. Then they'd shrink back against his teeth. Older and older he'd get. His hair would dry and twist and shrink until it looked like a badger's bottom. His skin would hang in folds. Turkey neck and bingo wings would be the least of his worries. Even old Hornbeam would look better than this – William Deforest wouldn't stand for being made drunk by some old man and falling downstairs on the way to—

'Another?' Hornbeam's eye was at his heart, his breath was on his neck.

Will swayed and crumpled. Strange memories invaded his mind. Archie Trice, was his last thought. Old Archie. *I remember …*

From the frames of a dozen photographs the sporting young millionaire looked down under his domed glass ceiling over the unconscious form of the Saturday odd-job boy. With difficulty Mr William Deforest James Hornbeam arranged his ancient bones beside his intended victim. Hooking his rucksack from under his stool, with shaking hands and dimming red eyes, the old man perused Will's wallet. 'William Dudgeon, Pilchard Inn, Lisle Island.' The eyes rolled and turned up. 'A publican's son – bah!'

The old man lay still and the sleepers slept, the fountain plinked, the fishes flickered gold in their blue pool, and the wisteria outside hung down as though to enfold Sleeping Beauty's palace. Not so beautiful, Hornbeam's narrow chest rose and fell. And at last Mike the barman found what he'd wanted in the cellar, and wondered what had taken him so long.

Soon a change came over the faces of the sleepers. One of them rose groggily, clutched a stool and went out. The other slept on, ruddy and peaceful, as Mike clumped up the cellar steps and scratched his head at the sight of him.

Mantha

'Chapel of Rest', read the faded sign over the door. A freshly painted sign in gold and black announced 'NETTLEFOLD & DAD: FUNERAL DIRECTORS'. Just inside the door an old sign waited by a bin. 'NETTLEFOLD & DAUGHTER: FUNERAL DIRECTORS.'

A deep silence rested over the deserted reception area and over the green-tiled room beyond, over the benches, cabinets and lockers, where a prone form waited under sheets. A dark-haired girl in a white apron entered the room briskly. She raised the sheet, curled her lip, called out, 'Beamer – where are you?'

At last the silence was broken by the sound of shuffling steps. An aged figure tottered into the room and looked around in bewilderment. It licked its lips and looked at its hands. 'I'm sorry, I don't—' It stopped. 'What's happened to my voice?'

'Hornbeam, don't just stand there.' The dark eyes swept over the old man, almost, it seemed to him, contemptuously. 'You'll get three caskets dressed and made up today, or my name's not Mantha Nettlefold.'

'I – fell over on the ferry.' The rusty voice creaked like a rotten door. 'I couldn't go home like this. I found this card. It says "Nettlefold & Dad".'

'Yes, and there won't be much of the business left if you swan about falling over on ferries when there's work to do, and you *know* how hard I've been trying.' Mantha put her hands on her hips. 'It's mean of you, Hornbeam, and where's the list?'

'List?' the voice trembled.

'The Order of Work – oh!' The black hair switched by in annoyance, returning with a clipboard, which was thrust at him. The old man took it. His dim eyes scanned it before it clattered to the floor. 'My name's Will. Will Dudgeon. I thought—' A fit of coughing seized the hollow chest. 'I – thought – you could tell me, what's – going on.'

'Beamer, if you're going to be peculiar today I'll have to get Dad to help me.'

The old man started as if noticing the man at the sink for the first time. 'Mr Nettlefold? Something's happened. I was doing the flowers – and I woke up, and I looked like this.'

'Asleep on the job again, Hornbeam?'

'I'm old,' the figure wailed. 'I can't walk and I feel like I'm ninety!'

'Hornbeam, have you been drinking?'

'Yes,' the figure gasped. '*A pink cocktail!*' The hands grasped at Mr Nettlefold. 'Please, you've got to help me—'

'Hornbeam, you've always looked like this.'

The hands grew excitable. 'That's just the thing, I *haven't*—'

'I could've sworn I'd seen to this one already.' Mantha's dad detached himself and considered the form under the sheet. 'When's he scheduled?'

'Tomorrow.'

'I thought—'

'Check the list.'

'Hornbeam?' Mr Nettlefold snapped his finger and thumb. Unsteadily the old man supplied him with the clipboard.

'Give him a comb-over and powder his face, that'll have to do,' the girl said. 'They brought in his clothes, but someone's lost them. I've had to use Hornbeam's mourning suit. How you managed without me, I don't know. The business'd go down the pan if I wasn't here; didn't join a moment too soon.'

'You could've finished school,' Mantha's father demurred.

'And have nothing to inherit? You'd be bankrupt without me. You've got no *systems* in place, you're not *organised* – look how much extra business the advertising's bringing in.'

'You might've completed your exams.'

'Nettlefold & Dad needs me now.'

'The change of name—'

'A good gimmick. Let's go through new appointments.'

Frisking out a large ledger, the Great Organiser looked interestedly through its pages. '"Order a casket in the comfort of your own home". Might have to change that slogan – why can't they come into the shop? Anyway, there's a Mrs Richards, at Rendel Grove, wants to book a funeral. Hornbeam, you can take that one, and for goodness' sake take the catalogue this time.'

Mantha turned. With a soft sound like falling dust Hornbeam collapsed, his chest doubling on to his legs, his legs lying down like pack animals, his head meeting the tiles and bringing Mantha to her knees.

'Beamer, what is it?' Mantha shook the fragile body. 'Dad, is it one of his turns?'

'Loosen his collar. I'll get his anti-convulsants.'

Mantha recoiled from the stringy neck. 'There, there,' she soothed. 'You'll be better after your medicine.'

Hornbeam's body convulsed, spinning on the tiles in a horrible parody of the break-dancing he'd once enjoyed. 'A pink drink,' he croaked, his reflection in a clinical cabinet staring back at him – an old man having a seizure on the floor. 'I woke up with hands like this.' He brandished his claws. 'I got up and my feet wanted to walk here. I fell over three times – I'm *thirteen years old*.'

'Here. Open his mouth.' A glass and two capsules materialized.

'You.' Mantha recoiled again, this time from the blue-grey gums. Then she recalled her business: dealing with those that were – down. She hooked out the false teeth and posted the pills past the rank breath in the throat.

'Well done,' said her father. 'You'd almost think—'

'Shut up, I'm not his nurse. Get him out of here.'

•　●　•

The medication down his throat and his little 'turn' seen to, and his supposed recovery done and dusted some time ago, the old man lay in an ante-room, recuperating. Will Dudgeon, for it was he in the crumbling body of Hornbeam, wondered what they used the room for. In a corner rested a musical instrument of some sort. It might be a bassoon, Will thought. On the door hung an unusual coat made of dog's hair. It came from Vietnam. The label with these two bits of information on it hung dismally out of the sleeve. From the wall at the base of his bed a ceiling-high poster of Jack Nicholson in *The Shining* glared insanely down. If he'd had to collect three random objects, he couldn't have made them more bizarre. Will's eyes wandered. So long as he lay still it was fine, he was still thirteen and Will Dudgeon. The moment he tried to move, or saw a bit of his body, it wasn't. Will Dudgeon lay very still indeed. Either he'd aged amazingly quickly, *or Hornbeam had stolen his life.*

They had to have swapped bodies. It was impossible that they both had this disgusting sack of bones to move around in. Will raised a claw. He could get very upset. Immediately he thought about it, he got very upset. You usually got a bit of warning about the end of the road – about sixty or seventy years' warning, if you were only thirteen. Usually you got to grow up and *do* things, have a house, car, kids, get a bald spot and a stomach, get ratty on weekends, before you disintegrated. Now none of that was an option. He must be about a million years old – a hundred and five at least. How close to curtains did that make him? Not to mention his parents ... Suddenly Will wondered if he'd somehow sped forward in time, and the bar at The Pilchard Inn would be manned by someone he didn't know, and his room at home would be—

'Where d'you think you're going?'

'I've got to go home,' Will croaked.

'You're in your room already, stupid.' Mantha's grin loomed close, then receded.

'You mean—' He lived here, in this chamber of horrors? A clock struck the hour, then another. 'Do I collect chiming clocks?'

'No, this is where we put all the rub—' Amaranth swallowed. The black eyes dropped, then confided, 'The point is, we're restructuring the business.'

'We are?'

'Yes, and you're on *my* side, Beamer.' She glared at him, tapping her fingertips on opposing elbows with her arms folded, waiting for him to jump up and join

16

her, as though he hadn't just had some kind of brain-threatening 'turn'.

Yet 'Beamer' was, it occurred to Will, a pretty friendly kind of name for a corrupt old bag of bones. The way his boss treated him, clearly they weren't best mates – how could they be? She might as well be best mates with a toast-rack. But she wasn't afraid of the evil eye that was Hornbeam. Quite the reverse. Amaranth Nettlefold, Executive Director of Nettlefold & Dad (as her title appeared on the business card he'd found in his – Hornbeam's – pocket), was clearly pretty feisty – the feistiest thing he, Will Dudgeon, had seen since … well, since his mum had got on her high horse about the revised school bus route ignoring the connection with the Lisle Island ferry. And now there was nothing for it – he, William Daniel Dudgeon, had better *be* 'Beamer' for a while. It wasn't like he had a choice.

'How – how long have we been working together?' he croaked.

'You're so funny. For ever.'

At least he could pump her for information about the old man. Figure out a way to get his own body back. 'And have I *always*—'

'No time for being old. I want you back out there taking orders.' Bending swiftly, she stripped Will's blanket from under him. He spun out on to the floor like a top, scattering pens from his pockets.

'Eeuw, you stink of formaldehyde.'

17

'But I don't—'

'Mrs Richards. Two forty-five. Don't be late.' Avoiding any contact with her slightly-creepy-but-usually-biddable assistant's claws, Amaranth Nettlefold, Mantha for short, shoved the bookings file and the casket catalogue at him. 'We're beating last year's sales figures by a mile already, and we're going to keep it up so's *I* can present "Nettlefold & Dad" to the Funeral Directors' Conference in April. No use rubbing your head, and don't even try those red eyes.' The fine black eyebrows arched sardonically. 'I know you rub soap in your eyes so's you can get off dressing the caskets, but this is serious. I'm *relying* on you, Hornbeam.'

'Hornbeam' Takes an Order

The bus jolted along Rendel Avenue. Will had wondered whether one of the shiny black stretches in the company garage might take him to his appointment, but they were called 'hearses', apparently, and were only used for ferrying the departed – who were the only ones, it occurred to Will, who wouldn't care how they travelled. Instead he'd gathered his ancient bones and fallen inside a number ninety-three bus. All the seats were taken. He'd glared at a couple of ten-year-olds, but they'd glared back and giggled.

No one had got up for him until the stops and starts had thrown him down in the aisle. Then a man almost as ancient as himself had stood up and offered his seat. For a moment Will had felt insulted. Then his knees had reminded him he was old.

He'd sat and regarded his sagging yellow cheeks in the flat stare of the bus window. People moved away from him. They saw he was ugly and old. No one felt sorry for him. He shouldn't be so ugly. He had no right coming out and about, no right at all, looking so downright offensive.

Still, a whole new side of the scheming nightmare that was Hornbeam had been revealed, Will thought, by the previous interview with Mantha. Now it was up to him, Will, to try to probe and use his eerie kidnapper's weaknesses to undo whatever had been done. Maybe 'kidnapper' wasn't quite the right word, but what else could you call a person who'd stolen your body? More worrying than anything else was the thought of *his own body and what it might be up to, presumably under Hornbeam's direction*, if they had, as bizarrely seemed likely, somehow swapped carcasses—

'Mind out, you silly old fool!'

Will ducked as a man with a box pushed past him. 'Sorry, I didn't—'

'I've come from the vet, obviously.'

'We oldies don't see things coming, do we, dear?' a kindly woman across the aisle sympathized. 'No need to be rude,' she added to the man with the box.

'Got to keep him still, see? Bad enough that he's on the bus. No telling how much stress he's been under.'

'What is it?' Will asked politely.

'Pedigree Zambezi croc.'

'Is there such a thing?'

The man looked at Will testily. 'Keep your 'ands off his box.'

The long avenue that was Rendel unfolded in a series of jerks that brought Will's purple nose within a whisper of the chrome rail of the seat in front of him, then rocked back the crumbling vertebrae in his neck as the driver braked and pulled away, braked and pulled away, and the bus stops grew distant behind them.

It had been hard enough to sort the limited change in Hornbeam's limited pockets as he'd got on, until he'd found a bus pass. Now Will found his eyes growing dim at the sight of the trees and shops lurching by. His neck snapped to and fro, his chest heaved to snatch enough breath, his legs began to tremble, his feet to grow cold, as if they weren't even there. Forget the bus pass, he'd take youth and a hassle to get on the bus without paying full fare, *even though he was only thirteen* (hold that thought) every time ...

Meanwhile the boy and girl opposite him had begun to whisper and giggle. Will felt his turkey neck grow hot, his jowls begin to quiver in outrage. His heart began to hammer. Didn't the fact that he was as old as the pyramids and not able to help it count for anything? Finally they were doing impressions. Will felt his head. It was horrible – nothing but bone and scalp. And something crusty. So a pigeon had blessed his head on the way to the bus stop – was it *his* fault signals reached his brain in slo-mo, and he never even felt the plop?

Suddenly Will remembered he should get off. Gathering himself up like a piece of old furniture, he swayed down the aisle to the driver, elbowing a man in the ear as he pressed the bell and falling backwards on top of a woman in a check coat as the bus lurched to a halt.

'He has hit me!' she howled from somewhere underneath him. 'This man, he hits me and—'

'I *fell* on you.' Will got up with difficulty, but the wailing only increased.

'This is the man!' The check coat grew hysterical in a thick Italian accent. 'This is the man who sits on me and hits me – oh, oh, I am damage to my stomach, and in the chest, here and here, and this – *this* is the man!'

'Sorry, I'm really sorry …'

'And he is crush me in my seat when he hits me in the head with his arm, and I am damage in my chest, my stomach …'

Stumbling up to the driver, Will gasped, 'Rendel Grove?'

'Passed it half a mile back.'

'But you said you'd tell me!'

'Let you off here, if you like.'

Will dismounted from the bus like a pillow tumbling off a bed. Sagging away down the road, he passed his fellow passengers stuck in traffic and watching his non-progress from the bus windows with a kind of enjoyment. Over their heads, a black-and-white check sleeve accused him audibly: 'There he goes with no care in his world of who he crush! *That* is the man who sits on me and hits me in my stomach, and in my head, and here, and here, and here …'

Will drew adjacent to the boy and girl gigglers. They made faces as he laboured by. Still laughing over an old geezer with a bird-dropping down the back of his collar? In the biggest voice he could muster, which came out oddly cracked and skipped a register or two in the middle to become an energetic screech, hopping up and down with rage, he yelled, 'SO I'M OLD, SO WHAT? SUCK IT UP!'

He turned to find a woman in black waiting quietly behind him.

'I see you're from Nettlefold's. My name is Mrs Richards.' She extended a gloved hand and opened the door of her car. 'Mr Hornbeam, I suppose.'

• ● •

The living room was a silent tribute to the life of Bartleby Richards. Bartleby Richards, head of local charitable organization the Tridents, receiving a cheque on behalf of an animal charity. Bartleby Richards, grinning down with a giant marrow behind his Best Small Allotment trophies. Bartleby Richards, retiring as the longest-serving butcher in town. Bartleby Richards, Town Councillor. Bartleby Richards, devoted husband, and father to Shawnie and Dovecote Richards.

'Isn't – Dovecote an unusual name?' husked Will through his tea and cakes.

'Dove, of course, we called her Dove.'

Will waited tactfully. 'Until?'

'Until she changed her name by deed poll to Helen. Myself, I always preferred Dove.'

'So the casket's for …?'

'Bartleby, of course.' Mrs Richards brought out a handkerchief. 'My dear Bartleby. Passed away at fifty-five. And all because of a sausage.'

Will felt a strange sensation passing up from the base of his withered stomach to the top of his light-headed brain. Several seconds passed while he fought it. Finally the irony of a butcher dying because of a sausage produced a kind of gurgle from his throat.

'I suppose you find that funny.'

Will turned the pages of the casket catalogue and carefully smoothed down the place Mantha had thoughtfully marked for him earlier with a sample order of service. 'With an oak casket,' he read, 'you can be sure of quality. How did you know I was there?' he added.

'Where?'

'The bus stop.'

'I was checking the shop window. Bartleby's Butchers, The Parade?'

Will turned the pages quickly with his claws. Best draw a veil over the shouting incident.

'That outburst of yours. At the bus.'

'Forgot to take my tablets today,' Will mumbled. 'With the teak casket, we can offer brass handles—'

'Bartleby had his outbursts,' Mrs Richards

24

remembered, dabbing her eyes. 'Rocky Road biscuits? I made them last night.'

Will didn't mind if he did. Rocky Road was one of his favourites.

'He had outbursts in town council meetings,' Mrs Richards went on lugubriously. 'Outbursts at Shawnie and Dove. Outbursts at that nice young man at the shop. Outbursts at the sausage machine, which was, of course –'

'Don't upset yourself.'

'– the end of – all his – outbursts.'

Will swallowed down another irresistible bubble of mirth from his stomach. He really should pin her down to a choice of casket. Perhaps the order of service might make him feel more miserable. Or maybe the—

'I'm really quite glad we won't have to put up with it any more.'

'The sausage machine?'

'The outbursts. Shawnie and Dove – Helen – are coming down with their partners for the wake, and we're having a jolly good knees-up. I said, we'll have sausage rolls dyed pink if we like, and that nice young man, Mister James, he can do anything he likes with the shop and have a drink on me, if he wants to.'

'We can collect from the mortuary in our hearse,' Will read. 'Of course—'

'Pink,' said Bartleby Richards's widow firmly. 'We'll

have pink and red and yellow flowers in the hearse, and a pink hearse, if we can get one.'

'Pink – as in sausages?' Will blinked.

'As in pushing the boat out, and to blazes with his old saving money. And I've checked the shop window, and I like it, and young Mister James, he uses fresh parsley round the joints, not old plastic parsley like Bartleby.'

Will felt they were getting off the point. 'Shall I put you down for the best casket we've got? And a full-on riot of flowers? And some really plush wreaths, gold-edged order of service, full dress for three funeral directors and all the trimmings?' He jumped up excitedly. 'A really wicked, wedged, full-on, top-dog, super-fine funeral, best and plushest in the terrace, on the block and in the world?' His voice cracked. 'Cos we can do that, we can, Nettlefold & Dad.'

'You've got a funny way of putting it – but yes.' Mrs Richards tucked away her handkerchief. 'The fact is, Bartleby's dead, and I've just got to—'

'Suck it up?'

Amanda Richards smiled. 'Why don't you leave me your card?'

The Vault

'… and she just rang up and ordered the *premium oak casket* and the Four Star Funeral with all the trimmings and said how helpful he was, how he'd understood immediately, how much he'd cheered her up …'

'Tight-fisted lot. Must've prised open the cheque book somehow.' The rumble of Mantha's father's voice interrupted her breathless astonishment.

'Goodness knows how he did it.'

'Must be his charm.'

Mantha giggled.

Will closed the shop door behind him and silently crossed to the cold room to earwig on their congratulatory conversation a little better. A puff of pride grew in his chest at the thought of Mrs Richards having ordered the best of the best, and even before he'd got back!

'And here was me thinking he was useless,' Mantha went on. 'He can have a funny turn every day, if he brings in orders like this.'

'Don't need gas for this one, do we?' Mr Nettlefold asked.

'The skin's fine. Just get the make-up.'

'What about padding?'

'Really, Dad, you're so out of touch. Anyway, it's five to five. You've got the Smithson appointment.'

Will flattened himself against the wall, but he needn't have worried – moments later the sound of Mr Nettlefold exiting through the Chapel of Rest and the garage died on the last bang of the last intervening door. The growl of the sleek grey Bentley reversing into the main road told Will that he was alone with Mantha.

Not that he was about to interrupt whatever gruesome procedures she was involved in. Some things were better left fuzzy. He didn't *want* to know. Once he knew, he'd never be able to un-know – then all his jokes would be ruined.

Amanda Richards had liked his jokes. When he'd begun spinning comforting images of Bartleby, Butcher, looking down from a giant picnic in the sky, she'd laughed to think of him choking over inferior meat products. Will had grown bolder and soon they were picturing Bartleby's reincarnation as a red-faced baby wanting meat pies, only to imagine his growing old and pompous, to blow a fuse once again over the odd runty sausage which *would* become jammed in the machine … Finally Will had suggested that Bartleby might be reborn as a pig, or as a meek and kindly shepherd. Amanda had liked the first idea. They'd had a second cream cake each on the strength of the forgiving image of Bartleby, Butcher, being born as a pig.

It was a lovely thought. And he had a talent for them. Death was the family business, after all, and it occurred to him that it wasn't all bad. Didn't those who were unlikely to dial for a pizza ever again at least get the chance to ditch their angina and carbuncles at last, carbuncles that were as painful as his were? Whatever carbuncles were. Will smiled grimly to himself. His first and only priority *was to get his young – his own – body back*, and with that, and only that, in mind he was about to get down and serious …

'Beamer, is that you?' A cold draught came in at the jamb as Mantha's eyes bored through the door. 'Don't just stand there then – I've got another little job for you.'

No way was he about to be *her* punchbag again. He had bigger fish to fry. Leaving the door to the cold room ajar, Will shrank away down some steps that had escaped his attention until now, but which opened invitingly in front of him into a fragrant, red-lit darkness.

• ● •

A massive spider plopped on to the open page of the curious yellow ledger that he'd found in a creaking drawer. Laying it gently aside, Will began to trace 'The Oddities' with a shaking finger.

The Oddities were a long list of names, some dating back into prehistory – a hundred and eighty generations to be precise – to the time of Stonehenge, as an untidy hand had noted on the first page. The names grew stranger and stranger. Aelric, Flag, Mekel – who were they when they were at home, as Will's mother was fond of asking. Later listings including Michaels and Johns, Edwards, Edwins and Earnests, and even Arthurs were OK. But what about Omars and Ulrics, and – here – even an Archie?

The spider darted across the page he wanted to turn, but suddenly Will felt he wouldn't disturb it for anything; alone in this prison-like vault it felt like his only friend in the world. His senses seemed to have been heightened – maybe it was fear of the dead-sounding passages that stretched away from the only electric light into the darkness ahead.

It had been a wine cellar once. The single red light blazed above a shelf and probed long aisles stacked with coffins, instead of barrels. Beside the shelf a stuffed bear stretched out mildewed paws and gazed past Will with mild glass eyes that hadn't seen daylight in years. Will had brushed past its paw, and the drawer had shot out and had offered him the ledger, complete with magnifying glass.

He'd needed the magnifying glass. His eyesight was old and faded, like the bear's foot on which he rested. And there were some peculiar entries, better read sitting down.

The entry headed 'James Hornbeam, Sailor', for starters. Before it, another was headed 'Archie Trice –

Unsound'. Will wasn't so decrepit that he didn't remember *that* name. Archie the millionaire. Archie the owner of Lisle Island Hotel: his, Will's, place of work in what seemed like another lifetime. Funny that Archie should turn up here and – turning the page – even funnier, *his own name in spidery capitals*, 'William Daniel Dudgeon', with 'Good Prospect' written beside it!

Will felt his heart perform a somersault; he reached for the pills in his pocket and downed a couple. In a moment or two he could turn back to 'Deforest Evans' and discover from a newspaper cutting that the famous mathematician had been found dead, with a broken glass in his hand, whilst walking in the West Country. A second article featured a boy who'd become a maths wizard overnight and had applied to go to Cambridge at the age of nine. Both cuttings were dated 31 October 1916—

'Playing with those old books again?'

Will started. 'Mantha. I – just got back.'

'Well done for the Richards order.'

Will shut the ledger. 'Oh?'

'As if you haven't been earwigging upstairs. Seen any Type Bs around here?'

Will looked around as though he knew what she meant.

'You've had a good check for them then.'

'Type Bs?'

'Anomalies.' Mantha's face glowed in the red light.

'Anom-a-whats?'

'Unusual situations. Bodies that can't be swapped, of course.'

'You mean clients?'

'I know about the ledger. You know what I mean.' Mantha looked at him coolly. For a moment Will thought he might fall down. Then the plink of a drop of water falling repeatedly into a puddle somewhere broke the silence, and Mantha reached across for the ledger. The pages seemed to fall in slow motion, to crash down and crush his thoughts utterly. 'Why – would I swap bodies?' Will managed at last.

'Only Hornbeam can do that.'

'But—'

'I know who you are.' Her finger found his entry. '"William Daniel Dudgeon, Pilchard Inn, Lisle Island." No use looking for a way to swap back to your own body either.'

'Why me?' Will croaked. It was the thing that had been bothering him most, apart from his bladder.

Mantha shrugged. 'Related to the rich Trices of Lisle Island, are we?'

'I work for them.'

'And you're fit.'

Will coloured.

'Healthy, I mean. Obviously he's got his reasons. He does a lot of research.'

'But if you knew I wasn't Hornbeam, why did you pretend I was?'

'We have to pretend, for Dad – I'm guessing he wouldn't like to know he's got an, um, *vampire*, on the books. Beamer'll come back and work for us, when –'

'I've popped my clogs?' Will quavered.

'– he's had his fun. There's always been a Hornbeam at Nettlefold's.'

Will looked into the mirror that the stuffed bear was holding, and VAMPIRE was the word that looked back. 'It's not *me* who's the vampire,' he whimpered. *I'm just the sucked-out shell.*

'He isn't exactly the blood-drinking sort, but you know what I mean,' concluded Mantha briskly, as though she were passing on a recipe. 'Let's get the Type B coffin handles, and get out of this stinking vault.'

'He's sucked my life away … how could you work with him … I'm thirteen, I've lost everything—'

'Beamer goes fishing sometimes. He might even throw you back.'

'How,' Will demanded, 'if I croak in the meantime? How will he throw me back?'

Detaching his claws from the ledger and replacing it under the bear, Mantha moved him on.

But Will was desperate now. 'How does he do it? What does he put in that potion? How would *you* know what he does and doesn't do?' Will raved weakly. 'What are you, five thousand years old?'

'Let's get you upstairs and into bed.'

'Shut me up in that room, you mean.'

'Let's get upstairs,' Mantha said.

'But where's the boys he's swapped with, the ones who are old and …?'

'Dead? We bury them at Nettlefold's, of course.'

The coffins lining both sides of the vault took on a new and sinister aspect. 'Is there one for …?'

'Free burials for employees at Nettlefold's is just one of our new perks. I'm having an eco-burial. I think we should set an example and do some straight talking in the trade, don't you? "A Green Way To Go", that's the text of my speech to the conference. You can hear my speech if you like; there's only three weeks to go.'

Will hauled his sorry hide up the steps. 'Can't wait,' he said.

• ● •

So the horrible vampire Hornbeam, or whoever he really was, had been skipping from body to body down the ages like a pirate boarding ships. How could Amaranth, a young girl, not care about the shipwreck of lives like his own? Will felt overwhelmed with bitterness. He actually began to cry out of pity for himself, before someone told him to 'can it, or stand aside'.

It wasn't the politest post office queue in the world, but it was the one he was in for his pension. The head-spinning information of the day before had given way to a restless night in which his complaining body had got him up to go to the toilet three times. The last time, he'd had a tussle with the dog coat on the back of his door, before finding his way back into bed.

Mantha had been silent over breakfast. Silent over the order book. He hadn't been able to get anything else out of her except a terse command to sort wreaths.

Sort wreaths? With his life ticking away? He'd managed to slip out when the bin men came, and had made his way down to the post office.

Still snuffling to himself, he'd joined the end of a queue and had waited fourteen minutes before he realized that the figure in front of him was a cutout advertising the Lottery. His dim eyes made even simple things difficult. He cried into his musty old coat a bit when he found out his mistake. Then he moved to the end of a long Monday-morning pension line, feeling foolish under the CCTV eye that watched his every move. Telly news blared over the shop counter. A boy had gone missing for a day and a night, then had come back and wrecked an island.

The post office queue shuffled very slightly forward, as Will reached the conclusion that Mantha herself was an Oddity. What else could explain her heartlessness? 'I lost the whole of my life and she doesn't even *care*,' he muttered. 'Look, look at my hand!' He held up a claw to the man in front. 'I'm falling apart – would *you* like it?'

'Shut it, granddad,' the man returned rudely.

The pension book he'd found in his pocket had given him the hazy beginnings of an idea, an idea that centred on an immediate return to Lisle Island to reclaim what was his – an idea that began with money for the bus and the sea-tractor as there was no way he could walk so far again. The very cells in his body seemed to be breaking down. The aggravations of old age were so much worse than he'd thought. Approaching the post office counter at last, somehow he dropped his glasses. He hadn't even meant to get them out.

A girl in a short skirt with a torn hem and black leggings bent to pick them up. How easily she bent, Will thought enviously. No major engineering works required to crank the old flanks into gear.

'Here,' she said kindly.

'Cheers.' Will dusted them on his overcoat. He always felt cold these days.

Cashier number eight, please, ordered the queuing system.

When he'd been sent from counter six to counter eight, Will finally brought out his book. 'Hi, I need to get some pension.'

The man in the white shirt returned the book. 'Not at this branch you're not.'

'What d'you mean?' Will's voice cracked.

'You need Rendelsham post office, and you should have a number.'

'A number?' Will squinted to make himself understood. Squinting seemed to help.

'Automated withdrawal number,' the post office man repeated.

'Look, I just need some dosh. It says I get dosh every week.'

'At Rendelsham, not here. Next!'

'Please,' Will begged. 'I just need to catch a bus.'

'Take a fifty-eight to the crossroads. Post office is on your right.'

'Please, I'm a pensioner, aren't I? Takes me ages to cross the road.'

'Can't help you, I'm afraid.'

'How'd you like a stick in your face? That's what it's like when you try to get up and your arms are all over the place. How'd you like to miss the kerb and fall over? Or –'

'That'll be all. Good day.'

'– or a dog biting your non-existent backside cos you're not fast enough to run away from it, how'd you like that?' Will screeched, losing it completely. He threw his stick over the glass with a lucky effort, and a whole bunch of alarms went off.

In the mêlée an arm steered him firmly towards the door. Struggle as he might, he couldn't get away. As suddenly as they'd started, the alarms cut out.

'It's my grandfather. He's confused,' Amaranth Nettlefold announced to the floor of the startled post office from the door. She squeezed his arm. 'He's so sorry – aren't you, Granddad?'

'I'm a hundred and seven,' Will croaked.

'And?' Another squeeze.

'I'm sorry to put a crimp in your day.'

The Crunch

Next day found Will waiting in the office after breakfast. At last Mantha's father entered, surprised. 'Hornbeam – what can I do for you?'

'Mister Nettlefold, I'm going to level with you—'

'Keep it up; this new way of talking's going down a storm with clients.'

'The thing is, Mister Nettlefold—'

'Roger.'

'Roger, is that – I could do with some dosh.'

'Your allowance is paid into the bank via BACS. That's been all right until now?'

'Cool, but now I don't want these BACS things, I want some cash.'

'Well, really, Hornbeam, you only have to say.' Mr Nettlefold threw down some fivers. 'Fill in a petty cash form whenever you're ready. You've got the vet's at ten.'

'The vet's?'

'Mr Hargreaves down at Paddy Paws has passed away and the family want to make the necessary arrangements. I'm going that way myself – I'll give you a lift.'

As they swept along in the stately grey Bentley the autumn leaves gathered in whorls and threw themselves down between long avenues of greying beeches. The mad pulse that beat in Will's heart – *get body back, get body back* – grew wilder as they neared Paddy Paws vets, which was yet another thing that stood between him and an immediate return to Lisle Island, where he assumed that Hornbeam was living the life of a boy named William Daniel Dudgeon.

It turned out to be the wrong location. Departed vet Mr Hargreaves's house was three miles away over the golf course. The Bentley had swept away, so Will had to suck it up and wait for a taxi summoned by the green-coated receptionist. He himself had taken the booking, so there was no one to blame but himself. Just as he was thinking of abandoning the whole thing and making his escape, the receptionist smiled. 'Taxi won't be a minute.'

'Cool.' Will shifted uncomfortably.

She looked at him. 'Would you like a drink?'

'Am I coughing?'

'Just a bit.'

The waiting-room shelves were stacked with dried feeds for animals, pesticides and leads. Two chairs away from Will a lady with a yapping basket on her lap was talking to a boy with a rabbit. 'Yes, and someone went mad in the hotel and smashed all that lovely bar having a party. They rode motorbikes through the fountain, they say, and all over those lovely carpets. Then they went down to the Pilchard – your rabbit's nice, what's his name?'

The boy squirmed. 'I don't tell everyone.'

'My dog's Daisy May. She's eighteen, but she's got a lump.'

'All right then – Ruggles.'

'Ruggles. That's a fine name for a rabbit.'

It was a very large rabbit.

''Scuse me,' Will said. 'You said the Pilchard Inn – did they rubbish that as well?'

The woman in the tartan coat turned to him. 'The publican was involved in an argument and a lot of the glasses got smashed. He was on South West News. Apparently it was his son and his friends. The hotel was the worst – young people these days ... Goodness only knows why they had to destroy the place.'

'Maybe there was a reason,' Will said, feeling sick.

'Maybe they never meant to,' added the owner of Ruggles. 'Maybe they were enjoying themselves and went a bit over the top.'

'Mrs Barnes and Daisy May?' the receptionist announced.

'Listen to me, trying to keep my mind off the subject.' Mrs Barnes's hands shook as she rose with the basket. 'I'll hand her over and go, if you don't mind. I've spoken to the vet already.'

Will felt he needed the toilet for the fourth time

already that morning. Eventually he found a white cubicle just as a young vet entered. It wasn't a loo at all! Instead a familiar basket rested nearby on a table covered in surgical instruments.

'Mr Barnes and Daisy May? Did you wish to stay for the procedure?'

'I'm not Mr Barnes.'

'In that case, Mrs Barnes has expressed a wish that someone should stay with her dog. She couldn't bear to stay, herself. Would you mind?'

Cupping Daisy May's head in his hand after her initial injection was easy. It was the gaze of Daisy May that Will found particularly hard to bear. He couldn't avoid it. It wasn't all right. There was no way to *make* it all right. Soon his own life would be over. His eyes would grow milky and his gaze far-seeing, just like the little dog's. What had he done with his life? Could he honestly say he'd made the most of it, even in his own body? Been as kind as he could have? The least selfish? Not grumped when his mother got him out of bed to help with the orders on Sunday?

Suddenly he knew what he had to do. 'I'm late for a grief-counselling appointment,' he apologized. 'I'm an undertaker. I have to go.'

'Thank you for your help,' the young vet said gravely.

Will signed a form and left the building. Stepping into a waiting taxi, he swept down the avenue of beeches, nearer and nearer to a tartan coat crying on a bench.

'Stop the car. Let me out.'

'Aren't we going to Hacienda Hargreaves, The Avenue?' the driver queried.

'Give me two minutes,' Will said.

• ● •

'… and Daisy May's being put to sleep is really sad, I know, but it's only the beginning of the next thing that you're going to do in your life, and it's going to be amazing!'

'So you think I should take up bungee-jumping?' Mrs Barnes smiled through her tears, and the autumn leaves fell on her coat.

'Wear something tight if you do, and make sure your eyes don't pop out,' Will advised.

'I lost my husband as well, you see …'

'Which is why you need a new hobby. Take mine. I like to watch birds. Geeky, but so what? I never used to, but now I watch everything and tick them off, seagulls and cormorants and herring gulls and terns, loads of stuff, all from my bedroom window.'

'Where do you live?'

'Pilchard Inn, Lisle Island.'

'Oh, where the high jinks have happened. You must know all about it.'

'Been away, haven't I?' Will checked his taxi. It would wait. And so long as he had a say in it, he knew where he'd be going next. 'So you don't need to worry about old Daisy May – she'll be in dog heaven somewhere, doing the old keeping the neighbours awake with a bit of yapping.'

Mrs Barnes laughed.

They strolled a little way in silence, and the leaves scuffed rhythmically under their feet and made a riff that began to mark time to a tune, and the tune was very sad, and very old. 'We used to go for holidays in France,' Mrs Barnes remembered softly. 'And sometimes I used to imagine – I think I read it in a poem – that the lads lost on the beaches in the war had somehow come back as seagulls.'

Will imagined it. 'Airmen and sailors, pinching your chips.'

'You have cheered me up. Thank you so much.'

Job done. Will turned to go. 'Someone stayed with her,' he added. 'They stayed with her until she closed her eyes.'

Mrs Barnes nodded. 'Could we meet, sometime? You're such a nice man.'

Will blanched. 'I'm hideous and old.'

Mrs Barnes smiled. 'Inner beauty.'

No way. For a moment someone had made him forget how crumbly and ancient he was. Will waved, and she waved back, and the tumbling leaves closed around her and whirled the scene away, as at last he returned to his taxi.

'Chatting people up at your age – gross.' Amaranth Nettlefold sat waiting for him in the back seat. She wore a strange mourning outfit which featured purple cuffs. 'And anyway, you took long enough. We can't do Hargreaves now.'

'How did you know I was here?'

'The family rang. I put a trace on the cab. And you're not skipping off anywhere.'

'I can't hardly *walk*,' Will said.

'You know what I mean. You asked Dad for money when you failed to get your pension. You're so stupid, you could order a taxi on the firm anytime and get back to your stupid old home.' She rapped the back of the seat. 'Home, please', and the taxi started up.

'Keep checks on me, why don't you?' Will felt like having a massive row with her. His chest felt congested, as though he were drowning. When at last the coughing had subsided, they were almost back at Nettlefold's.

'Don't know what Dad's going to say. Missing an important account.' Mantha signed for the taxi and guided him up to his room. 'I'm going to ring Mrs Hargreaves. You'd better lie down. Want a drink?'

'Not from you.' Will turned away. Outside the sky was growing stormy, and rain began to speckle the roof of the Chapel of Rest. A single herring gull wheeled on the clouds gathering one above another, like buildings. Maybe it was a lost airman. Maybe it was just lost.

'What's the matter with you?'

Will found her little gloves on the bed; in a sudden passion he tore them to pieces and threw the pieces down. He lay back, exhausted. 'All *you* care about is the business.'

'Meaning?'

'You couldn't care less what's happened to me.'

'I don't know who you are,' Mantha said simply.

The publican got involved in an argument … lots of glasses got smashed … it was his son and his friends …

'Come home with me and I'll show you.'

'What?'

'Come with me,' Will repeated, hauling his body shakily upright in the bed. 'I'm going back where I came from to see what Hornbeam went and did to my body – my family.' He raised a shaking finger and tapped his poor, narrow chest. 'Come to Lisle Island – tonight. I'll show you who I am!'

Return to Lisle Island

That night the storm rose wildly. The wind whipped across the rooftops as Mantha turned over the Honda 250 in the courtyard behind the garage. 'Hop on before Dad realizes!'

'What?'

'I'm not meant to ride on the road!'

'You took your test?'

'Not yet! How old d'you think I am?'

He hadn't planned on going by motorbike. The hopping figure toppled, and with an effort hauled itself upright against the side of the old horse trough. The figure's reflection gazed up at it from the stagnant water inside. Behind its dark outline the clouds raced pell-mell over the moon.

The sight of his ancient body clad in biking leathers surprised even Will, himself. He looked like a giant stag beetle, or a crab in designer tights. Tottering across the cobbles was hard enough, never mind lifting a leg in the air.

'Hurry up and get on!'

Way easier said than done. At last he found a box to stand on and finally the leg was cocked, the ancient backside settled. Mantha kicked away the stand – 'Hold on!' – and then at last they were flying. Through the silent backstreets of the town, through the deserted outskirts, past the silent chippie …

'Which way?'

Will felt the wind in his teeth. He took them out and pocketed them. 'Head for the sea!' he screeched.

Of course. And now the dunes were building, and the bed-and-breakfast signs were beginning, and the tang of salt was in the air, and Mantha's hair flowed free – and there were the signs for Lisle Island!

'NINETEEN TWENTIES THEMED HOTEL. CROSS CAUSEWAY BY SEA TRACTOR ONLY AT HIGH TIDE.'

And there it was on the moonlit beach below, its canopy edged with salt-rime and its engine covered with a tarp – the strangely tall tractor with giant wheels that routinely battled the waves. Mantha ripped off the tarp and climbed aboard.

'Wha—'

'Tide's in. There's no other choice.'

'But you can't drive a sea tractor.'

'Can't I?'

Will wouldn't have bet on it, and neither would any other soul under that flying-cloud sky who saw Mantha clean off the points and prime the old diesel engine. In no time the canopy was rocking in its usual way, the engine roaring like a barely contained rocket as the red wheels began to grind round.

'There's sort of a road – a way it always goes.'

'Hang over the side, and watch for it then!'

A road under the sea, Will thought, as the giant wheels crashed into the water and the waves beat through them and under the wooden deck, never coming over it but threatening, all the same, to swamp the roaring tractor and extinguish it like some old-time dragon.

Will thought he saw jellyfish in the midnight water as they rattled and swayed along their way. It was enough, he thought, to wake the dead. Enough to wake all of Lisle Island. But no lights popped on in the dark hotel and the Pilchard Inn lay silent.

'How am I doing?' Mantha shrieked.

'Left a bit – past those rocks!'

The rocks looked like shark's teeth, the waves like a mouth waiting to snap up the tractor like a spicy titbit. Up and down they reared, the wheels churning great wakes of foam, their plunging lights startling night-feeders, crabs and anemones, sending flounders shooting away as if fired from a gun.

'Where's the causeway?'

Will looked down in despair. Soon they'd be in deep water. Finally he caught a glimpse of concrete, not a moment too soon.

'Over there! Right, right!' he gestured with flailing arms. And Mantha cranked the wheel and they lunged right, and the wheels gripped, and they steadied, and were saved.

Will checked progress over the side. Clear glimpses of concrete confirmed they were on the right track. 'Think we're going to make it!'

'No kidding!' The oil-grimed Mantha grinned.

Will looked back. Already the bike in the car park looked like a toy, the dim headland studded with occasional lights, like a land far away they'd never known. Spray soaked Will's leathers and dashed over the engine. Sparks went up from flying belts, and over all of it the stars looked down as the dark sea beat all around them and the bulk of the island frowned down. Will tasted every moment in his toothless old mouth, and he threw back his head and exulted – never in his young-old life had he *lived* as much, or so sharply!

'Hornbeam – you all right?' Mantha left the wheel to clap him on the back. His neck unlocked, and he gave thumbs-up, and could speak and breathe again. And now the little beach came in sight. Left a bit – right a bit! Now!

The wheels rose as the sea tractor clawed the moon, then settled back and bit the ramp. Now they were grating along gravel, now at last the roar of the engine echoed against the walls of the little harbour – and now it cut out and was still, and only the shriek of the wind deafened Will, and only Mantha's hair blinded him and even in the sea air smelled of lilies, and jasmine.

'Not bad going, we—'

'Get out!' She helped him down the ramp and up a set of stone steps into the lee of a road that wound steeply uphill.

'Maybe we s-s-should—'

'Put your teeth in.'

'Maybeweshouldgouptothehotel,' Will said, all at once.

'You live there?'

'No …'

'Thought you wanted to go home.'

The familiar pine trees at the approach to the hotel whipped and moaned in the wind. 'We won't be able to get in.'

'Who's there?' A lantern flashed above, between gusts. 'Is that you, Samuel Levett?'

'No, it's me, Will Dudgeon!'

Sam Levett was the usual sea tractor-man.

The lantern flashed closer. 'Doesn't sound like Will Dudgeon. You can stay away, if it is. And who's that with you?'

'Amaranth Nettlefold.' Mantha waited.

The lantern was with them now. Uplit by a swinging orange light, the face of housekeeper Mrs Rhymer loomed like a Hallowe'en pumpkin. 'Aren't you breaking your ASBO, or is it too early to take effect— Where is he then?'

'Who?'

'Will Dudgeon.'

Will took a deep breath. This was how it was going to be on his home turf until he could wring Hornbeam's neck and force him to exchange bodies back, and he wouldn't have the strength to explain every time, even if anyone would believe him.

'He gave me a message.'

'Oh, did he?'

'He wants to say sorry for anything he's done and pay for any repairs.'

'Anything? You mean everything. Early hours of the morning are a funny time for an insurance assessor to arrive, but I suppose you've come down from London. Step this way,' said Mrs Rhymer. She swung back. 'Did I see you driving the sea tractor?'

Mantha nodded.

'Who are you?'

'Mr Hornbeam's assistant.'

'Well, mind the steps, and come on then.'

· ● ·

The damage to the mirrored bar was heartbreaking. It wasn't just a few broken glasses left upturned in the troughs of lilies; it wasn't just that the fish were dead, or that their blue pool was criss-crossed with the bicycle tracks that led out through the patio doors into the muddy garden; it wasn't just that some kind of cherryade had been poured into the keys of the white piano; or that Mike's little cubby-hole had been filled with chairs and set light to: no, it was worse than that. The slender, silver statue of a dancing girl, a flapper, with her bobbed hair and svelte beaded dress, a statue that Will had always returned to after all the little jobs were done – the silver flapper had been beheaded and her lithe body chucked on the parquet. Instead of topping her gay dancing frame, her head now sat in the sand of an ashtray amongst the rancid cigar butts. Will picked it sorrowfully out. Who but someone filled with evil glee could have done this?

'Lucky for us the party moved on,' nodded Mrs Rhymer.

'Moved on?'

'To the Pilchard Inn.'

A thrill of fear struck through Will's heart. His poor mum and dad, and Polo the dog. 'When was this?'

'Yesterday morning. After I called the police.'

'The police?' said Will faintly.

'Then, let me tell you, they'd had – oh, yes – *quite* enough of us.'

'They?'

'Mr Will and his friends. And you can tell him I said so.'

'My mates are all in school,' Will blurted. 'They couldn't have done any of this.'

Mrs Rhymer eyed him. 'I don't know what kind of friends you've got, but can we get the assessment started?'

'Here's the forms,' Mantha said, handing her a funeral application pack. 'We'll need to take a tour on our own.'

'Don't let me influence you, I'm sure,' huffed Mrs Rhymer. 'The dining room's through there. You'll find the flowers in the piano and the cruet sets in the radiator. He kept shouting, "I'll wreck it if I want to, it's mine! I left it TO MYSELF!" and laughing and laughing. He laughed so much, he cried. Then he left on a quad bike he found in the garage – it wasn't even his.' Mrs Rhymer's nostrils quivered with indignation. 'The things he did to my kitchen. Left it to himself, indeed! I'd like to know how, 'less he's Mr Trice!'

Will looked around at the smashed and crazed photos of Archie Trice, which now reflected the once-elegant bar. For the first time he noticed a family tree in pictures. Archie's heir had been his cousin Henry, and *his* heir had been his son, Jonathan. Jonathan Trice was still the owner, Will noticed from the date, but the hotel was managed by a faceless group named Ambergris Holdings.

Now Will remembered he'd seen him, once. It must have been Jonathan Trice who'd visited the hotel one summer not so long ago, to announce redecorations. The old man who'd sat on the beach in a panama hat had winked at him once, he remembered. Also he'd coughed a lot in interviews on the telly news, and had to have been at least ninety years old …

'… seventy-nine and in failing health,' Mrs Rhymer concluded. 'They say he's got weeks, maybe less.'

'Has he made funeral arrangements?' Mantha asked.

Will glared at her. 'Who's next in line?'

'Mister Jonathan never married.'

'So who inherits?'

'Who knows? But it won't be the boy from the pub.'

• ● •

They wandered out into the garden. Below them the boathouse smoked quietly against the backdrop of the bay, as the fire inside it still smouldered. Beneath the boathouse a steep path wound down to Archie's private beach.

'Phew!' said Mantha. 'Major.'

Will felt sick. How could his body have led such a rout through bedrooms, kitchen and lounge bar? The extraordinary lounge bar jutted out over the swimming pool and had been one of Archie's most extravagant fantasies. He'd longed to be a pirate and had built the back end of a pirate galleon into the side of his lounge bar overlooking the sea. Hornbeam had apparently walked several employees, including Mike the barman, off a plank and into the swimming pool. Must have been a riot watching the little chambermaid named Anna sink, as she couldn't swim. Will felt rage, then disgust. He'd had enough of this now. 'Let's go home for breakfast.'

'What time is it?'

The cockeyed clock over the sundeck stood at eight forty-five. A door opened in the service quarters at the side of the building and a large voice rang out. 'These forms, they're not right! Mr Assessor! Where are you?'

'Quick, she's coming! Run!'

Escaping Mrs Rhymer's approaching form waving a handful of papers, they ducked away through the pines and hid in the first bunker on the nine-hole golf course beyond. 'We can cut over there to the Pilchard.' Will pointed. The crooked red roof of the pub stood out beyond the second tee.

'Remind me?' Mantha's perfect brow crinkled.

Will looked at her. 'My parents' place – where I *live*?'

'I'm sorry. It's hard for me to remember you're not Hornbeam.'

'It's easy for me. I just look at my hands and remember I'm thirteen.'

'No need to be like that.'

'How would you be, if you were suddenly a hundred million years old?'

'A slight exaggeration.'

Will rolled up his musty old waistcoat. 'Take a look at that sad-sack stomach and tell me you could forget.'

Mantha looked away. 'All right, you made your point. Take me home with you, and we'll figure out a way to get "you" back.'

• ● •

Home was already occupied, of course, by someone more than a little like himself. Apart from a terrified glimpse on first rising from the floor after the smoking pink cocktail that had started it all – back when he'd first fled the hotel and his feet had found their fumbling way to Nettlefold's – it was the first time Will had seen his body *whilst being outside it*.

'Duck!' He locked eyes with Mantha while over their heads his mother dusted toast crumbs off a plate for the birds. The kitchen window had been open and blocking their path to the door. But now it seemed like a good place to pause and assess the situation.

By rising carefully and looking round the side of the window, Will could see everything: his mother, frying bacon and eggs, the dog licking its lips at her feet. His own legs gave Polo a kick. 'Get outside, you old mutt.'

Polo whined and disappeared under the table – the only one of his family, Will could see, who wasn't likely to be fooled by appearances. Polo would never have acted so cowed with *him*. Good old Polo. He'd missed the liver-spotted spaniel so much.

'That breakfast ready yet?' Hornbeam lolled in his dad's chair by the range. Will's father's crossword table had been covered in jars filled with powders.

'I wish you'd let me clear that table,' his mother worried.

'Leave it,' Hornbeam growled.

'All right, but you're due down the station at ten, don't forget.'

'I don't need some old woman to remind me.'

'I'm your mother, and don't you forget it.' Will's mum clapped a plate of fry in front of the being she took to be her son. 'I don't know what's come over you lately, but get your breakfast down your neck; you're in a whole heap of trouble, my son.'

To Will's astonishment, Hornbeam sulked over a top breakfast.

'I'm not putting up with such dreadful behaviour,' his mother continued, stacking the dishwasher. 'I'm not afraid of you, and neither is your dad.'

'Watch out, or I'll *upset* myself,' Hornbeam sneered.

'You know that the psychologist said you need to keep calm till your next assessment.'

'Keep the kid gloves on, like she said, or I might go completely insane.'

'You just need to stop this behaviour.'

'You had me. Everything I do is your fault.'

'I don't think that's the way it works.'

'You don't know a thing,' Hornbeam said contemptuously. He wolfed his bacon and yolks and shovelled his egg white and toast on to the floor. 'Give that muck to the mutt.'

Mantha ducked as it came out of the window. In moments the back door opened and Polo joined them.

Will instantly seized his muzzle. 'Come away,' he signed, 'or he'll blow it.'

Mantha followed him; Will crawled away and made the garden shed before his joyful reunion with the only living soul who knew him straight away for who he was.

• ● •

His father wasn't there. It was all so confusing. Hadn't Hornbeam treated his, Will's, body to an ASBO? Maybe his dad was already down at the cop shop, filling in forms for his son. Will felt filled with pity for both his parents. The times he'd lain in bed whilst his mum slaved over pub dinners downstairs on a Sunday flashed before him. He'd never been as bad as all that, but still somehow Hornbeam seemed like an exaggerated version of his, William Daniel Dudgeon's, own selfishness. It wasn't a pretty picture.

Mantha shook her head. 'I don't know what's got into him. He's giving them such a bad time.'

'Welcome to my world.'

'I'm sorry.' Mantha covered Will's gnarled hand with hers. 'I'm so sorry.'

'Not your fault, is it?'

'I'm sorry,' she said again.

'Polo, down! He knows it's me – isn't it great he knows it's me?' Will hugged the dog as his only real friend. 'Your ears smell. You look like an old sock. Yes, you do. An old sock.'

'You always talk that way to your dog?'

'Only when he smells right. Yes. And how does he smell today, Mister Smelly Smellerson—'

'Talking of smells. Thought I niffed a rat,' quipped a voice familiar to Will.

'Hornbeam!' Mantha rose.

Will fought for breath within the chest of his ancient adversary, while his own body regarded him scornfully. There was something all wrong about it, like Frankenstein's monster. For a start, he himself would never stand that way – never talk to his mother like that. Where was she anyway? He had the strangest feeling he'd die if he met her, and she didn't know him.

Mantha set her jaw. 'Not this time, Hornbeam.'

'Not this time, Hornbeam,' Will's voice mimicked nastily.

'I order you—'

'Oh, I'm scared.'

'I *order* you to give WILLIAM DANIEL DUDGEON HIS BODY BACK – NOW!'

'Make me,' Hornbeam sneered. Mantha began to hit him. Easily fielding every blow, Hornbeam began to laugh. Holding both her arms together, 'Nothing to say, old man?' he crowed, kicking Will as he rose. His, Will's, body was good and strong, a very good body for a bully. Polo took an interest in one of Hornbeam's legs, but in no time he'd been booted away by one of Will's own trainers.

'You didn't have to kick him!' Will cried.

'Didn't have to bite me, did he?' Hornbeam threatened

a foot again. There was a real intention to hurt in his every move. 'No one gave *me* a break.'

'Here.' Mantha opened a fist sardonically.

'What?'

'The world's smallest violin, playing just for you.'

'In a hundred thousand lives, no one's cared for me.' The thirteen-year-old face darkened as Hornbeam remembered. 'No one's so much as given a twopenny-ha'penny curse for yours truly, or cared for me more than a horse—'

'Ridiculous self-pity!' snorted Mantha. 'Had a mother, did you, Hornbeam? Sure it wasn't a reptile? You'd better let me go, or I might say something—'

'Shut it.'

'I don't know much, do I, Hornbeam – or should I say Vampire King?'

'Who are these people?' a fourth voice demanded.

'Dad!' Will gasped.

'I don't know who you are, but I'm not your father,' said Mr Dudgeon, looking him up and down. 'Would you mind going round to the pub entrance? And in any case we're not open yet.'

'This old person and his grotesque sidekick have been invading our privacy,' sniffed Hornbeam.

'Journos, I suppose. This is private property. If you don't mind …?'

Dad, Will felt like shouting, hug me, don't show me the gate!

'All right,' said Mantha, 'we'll go quietly this time, but don't think you're getting away with it, Hornbeam.'

'Whatever you can possibly mean by that?'

'We've got the recipe, remember?'

'Whatever.' Still, Hornbeam wasn't unworried.

'Hornbeam? What's going on?' Mr Dudgeon demanded. 'Who are these people, Will? Will?'

Mantha pulled him away and they left on this note of uncertainty, Will sorrowfully overhearing his dad trying to question the cuckoo he thought was his son. 'There's more to this than meets the eye. Well, what are they *doing* here?'

'I don't know, do I? Shut it.'

'I'll give you shut it, my lad. We're due down at the police station in half a tick, and we'll be early, if you don't mind.'

'*You* be early, I'll be – rich!'

'No need to snatch the paper.'

'The devil, I don't. See the headline? The old man's died!'

'The old man?'

With a wild air of exultation: 'Now – now we'll see a few things! There's a few surprises waiting, hang me if there aren't! And won't *you* have to mind what you say to me!'

They'd taken a few steps towards the harbour, when suddenly Will turned back.

'Will!'

'No, I'm not letting him get away with it.'

Seconds later he roared from the side of the house on a quad bike he'd noticed there earlier. In and out of the garden hedge a few times, and Will had acquired an animal to herd, a Hornbeam – and he herded him ruthlessly up the hill and over the golf course, across the eighth tee, through the pines to Archie's hotel – the hotel that Will had felt so protective towards, without even quite knowing why.

They crashed through the foyer and into the lounge bar. Will dismounted with more righteous energy in his old bones than he'd felt in a long time.

'Walk the plank!' he croaked. 'You made Anna do it!'

'I'm young and strong,' sneered Hornbeam. 'Make me.'

Will saw that Archie's case of fishing rods had been shattered, and his prize trout line leaned out of it. With a sudden inspiration he whirled the rod around. 'I'll hook you like a trout!'

'Now hang on—'

'Like a trout, right through your nose!'

Will whirled the line above his head, and the hook glinted dangerously through the air.

'You'll have my eye out – mind that hook, will you?' Hornbeam backed away on to the plank and glanced towards the end of it, jutting from the 'galleon' window. 'Look, I'm in a position – shortly in a position – to make you very rich. Very rich indeed …'

Will advanced with the fishing rod. 'No kidding.'

'I – I can't explain just yet, but – look, I don't like heights …'

'Tell me about it, Hornbeam.'

'... and you wouldn't want anything to happen to *your own body*, would you?'

It was a good point. 'I'll risk it,' Will said. 'Walk!'

It wasn't an amusing option when you had to do it yourself, Hornbeam saw, too late. In a moment the fishing rod was nudging him along the plank and out over the swimming pool, the very rod he'd used to encourage everyone else to take the dizzying plunge. Far below swam the turquoise rectangle of the pool. There was a brief smudge of whirling trees and golfers before a final prod caught him between the shoulder blades and – youthful reactions or not –the cuckoo that looked like a Dudgeon fell like a stone towards the water ...

Surfacing like a star, he lay face down for precisely two and a half minutes while Will bellowed after him, 'Hornbeam, breathe! Hornbeam!'

It would be like him to drown out of spite. Three seconds later, the feather-light form of an old gent hit the water.

Will surfaced immediately. Somehow he towed the heavy young body towards the steps. Turning him over was harder, but suddenly Mantha was beside him. 'Work his chest!'

'You!'

'Come on, come on, come on!' She looked at him. 'Wait – here's your chance. He's unconscious. I know how to help you slip back into your own body, while he's out for the count!'

'Tell me!' Will panted.

'It'll mean letting him croak.'

Will hesitated. Hornbeam was blue around the mouth – *his* mouth – already. 'Why?'

'Only room for one.'

It seemed only just. 'Quick, what do I have to do?'

'Nothing.' She met his eyes over the drowned-looking body. 'Soon as he goes, you'll be sucked back in. Then you'll have seconds to breathe.'

'You mean—'

'With luck, you can save yourself.'

Will thought at lightning speed about doing nothing. For a brief window in time, the power to slip back into his temporarily vacant body lay with him – *his* power to push Hornbeam into his rightful place, the place where people who would never order a pizza again went, the place where Bartleby, Butcher, no doubt treated angels to sausages – but something in him hesitated, and Hornbeam opened his eyes.

Will cleared his airway, and the young oxygen-starved body took in a shuddering breath. Lucky for Hornbeam that his body was so strong.

'I let you off this time, but don't think you're getting away with it,' Will whispered.

'No,' smiled Hornbeam, with Will's lips. And lay back in his arms.

Business Intervenes

The trick was to con him into drinking the same stupid concoction that had started the trouble in the first place, and then drink some himself, Will thought. A strange taste in the mouth, a few minutes conked out beside Hornbeam, then he'd wake up in his own body again – and so would the horrible old bloodsucker. It would be a straight swap, the way it had been at the beginning, except that this time the boot, or the oldie's turned-up slippers, would be on the other foot …

'Drone, drone – Beams, are you listening?' Mantha paused, notes in hand.

'Will,' he corrected.

'Thought we agreed "Hornbeam" in the office, cos of Dad.'

'Whatever.'

'How much of this speech have you heard?'

'Since eco-coffins,' Will sighed, shifting in his office chair at Nettlefold's.

'Eco-coffins,' Mantha repeated, 'can be made of hand-crafted pine, or we can offer a bamboo casket or a moss-lined willow nest. And in addition to having a name to bring a smile to your lips when you most need one, Nettlefold & Dad offer a hands-on approach to Green Burials Maintenance. It's important people aren't upset –' Mantha put her hands on the desk in emphasis, her acid-green sleeves and mess of dark hair making her look a little like a willow nest herself. '– it's important people aren't upset by coming back and finding cows plopping on their uncle Rodney's plot three months later. At Nettlefold's we take a dim view of ruminants—'

'Rumi – whats?'

'Cows.'

'Don't think you need the "plopping",' Will advised.

Mantha crossed it out. 'Our "Green Angels" policy ensures a carefree visit to Auntie Ermintrude's patch of grass, which will be clearly marked on our Locate-a-Relative map—'

'Practising your conference speech?' Mantha's dad put his head round the door. 'Seen the papers? J.B. Trice has died. I want to bid for the funeral.'

Will swallowed. 'J.B. Trice? You mean—'

'It's a biggie. I've rung the estate. I want you both at Lisle Island on Monday to put in our price for the entire funeral. Of course, there'll be competition. But I'm confident you and Hornbeam can pull it off. There's a meeting at Throwbones Solicitors to read the will. Crammed with press, of course, so we've no chance of getting a look-in. Papers say that the mystery heir is about to be revealed.'

'But we've just got back,' blurted Mantha. 'From shopping, I mean. And anyway, don't *you* want to go?'

'Can't compete with Hornbeam's winning touch. I expect it's on the midday news.' Mr Nettlefold clicked it on. After a couple of items, sure enough, it came up:

Death of hotel magnate ... new heir to vast fortune not yet known ... estate liable to be in limbo for some time ... luxury hotel chain to be managed as usual ... odd events at Lisle Island probably triggered heart attack ...

Will didn't really take it in. Hornbeam's ravings about being rich, and his wild attempt to bribe him, Will – with what? – before he'd walked the plank, occupied every brain cell he had left. 'What's it all about?' he croaked, not sure if he was thinking or speaking. 'What's it ... all ... about?'

The wild trip to Lisle Island to reclaim his life already seemed like a dream. So had saving his own body from drowning. The sopping Hornbeam had smiled weakly up at him. Leave him, Mantha had insisted. He's got as much feeling as a wet fish. Really? Will had wondered. Really. Don't feel sorry for him. There'd be no point in staying, Mantha had insisted, unless they had a plan. Yes, they'd return when they had one. They had to regroup and think it through. That was the smart thing to do.

During the return crossing Will had kept his eyes

fixed on the pirate-ship-end of the lounge bar, and the plank sticking out of its window. The wet fish beside the pool would have recovered, would be down at the police station explaining itself. Great. Now he'd be fingerprinted, and would have a criminal record.

The ride back on the sea tractor with tractorman Sam Levett had proved to be a bit of an eye-opener in itself. ('That young Will Dudgeon made a name for hisself. Always been a bit of a tearaway. Now he thinks he owns the place.') Will had replied pretty coldly. It gave him a different view of himself as not quite as likeable as he'd thought …

They'd got back exhausted – or Will was – and had lain low the rest of the day.

Next morning Mantha had insisted on his hearing her conference speech. He hadn't seen the papers or heard the news until now. Now it seemed that Jonathan Trice, last in the line of Archie's heirs, had really, actually died – and he, Will, a young head on a crumbling body buried in the depths of an undertaker's offices, had been the last to hear of it.

One thing he didn't understand.

With no more Trices left to inherit how could anyone, least of all Hornbeam, become rich – very rich – out of it?

'Hornbeam, wake up, you've fallen asleep in front of the news!'

Now he was swaying in a pirate ship with Archies

manning the galleys, and pound notes for sails. 'Wha's – it about?' Will muttered.

'Hornbeam, you're dreaming! Really, if he wasn't such a hit with clients lately, I'd seriously think about putting him out to grass.'

'Try again,' Mantha laughed.

Will woke to find Mr Nettlefold's elegant, be-ringed hands rocking his shoulders again. 'You dropped off when I was speaking to you – Hornbeam!'

'Sorry I'm dozy. I'm a crumbly,' Will muttered.

'Never mind extreme age, you've still got charm.' Mr Nettlefold raised his eyebrows. 'A Mrs Barnes rang me to say how much you'd helped her, and I've never even heard of her. By the way, they want you back at Paddy Paws.'

'But the Hargreaves funeral was Tuesday,' Will remembered with an effort.

'It seems they want to retain you as a pet-owner's grief counsellor, heaven only knows why.' Mr Nettlefold clapped Will on the back. 'Can't help bringing in more business again, eh, Hornbeam? Take a nap if you want. Take as much time as you like.'

Will made an effort to get up, and at last got the old pulleys working. 'I'm just a bit stiff. I've been riding a motorbike.'

'At your age?' Mr Nettlefold laughed quite a lot. 'I should like to see you in leathers, Hornbeam. I jolly well should!'

He went out shaking his head, and every now and then a bellow of laughter rang out from the hollow depths of the cold room, as he remembered the image.

At Throwbones Solicitors

'Fetch me some number sixteens from the vault!'

'Your wish is my command.' Will felt more like a member of the Addams Family every day.

'And don't forget we've got Throwbones this afternoon!' Mantha added.

'How could I forget?'

The vault again – where the nameless coffins of Hornbeam's victims mouldered down the ages. But he knew where the number sixteens were this time. And the number seventeens and eighteens. He was becoming quite a handy undertaker's assistant – too handy by far. Coffin handles were the least of Will's worries. Uppermost in his mind was the fact that Hornbeam was probably still lording it at the Pilchard, terrifying his mum and dad, putting his boots on Polo, and now probably—

'Hurry it up, Beamer, we haven't got all day!' Mantha's voice seemed to curl around the door after him.

Will had submitted to being called 'Beamer' whilst in the office for Mr Nettlefold's sake only after a stiff argument.

The fact that he looked like a stooped old man, more like a 'Theophilus' or an 'Augustus', and not much like a 'Will' couldn't actually escape him, since the many mirrors at Nettlefold's told him as much every time he shuffled past them. One mirror in particular always seemed to show him in a very unflattering light. It had lacquered Chinese dragons curving around it, and he hated it quite a lot.

'Can't you move that mirror?' he'd said. 'Does it have to be in the hall?'

'You leave that mirror alone,' Mantha had told him darkly.

He'd even got used to soaking his teeth in a glass beside his bed at night. He slept lightly, and dreamed a lot, and had to gather his back and his legs together to stand up at all in the mornings. This was what awaited everyone, if they were lucky enough to live as long – everyone except the body-hopping Hornbeam. Most people had some fun in between being toothless at either end of their lives. Good thing he knew who he was. He had to keep reminding himself.

The stone steps down to the vault yawned beside the cold-room door. Stumbling down them with a torch, he re-entered the red-lit crypt that seemed to stretch in all directions.

Aisles of coffins – 'caskets' they were called in the trade – stretched away in storage racks waiting for relatives to choose them. Beyond the different models –'Superior', 'Sandlewood', 'Perfect Rest' – stretched dim lines of much older caskets. It was these that made Will shudder. And he had to walk between a particularly dim and musty row to get to the coffin handles.

At last he reached the draper's glass-fronted drawers labelled with the handle numbers

Wrenching out a couple of drawers and feeling ghosts prickling his skin and nerve-endings, raising the ends of his fluffy hair and making it wander in a draught that had sprung up from nowhere, Will made a grab for the handles and prepared to make a swift retreat.

Suddenly he dropped a number sixteen, which went ringing away on the floor.

It was while he was bending to pick it up that he stumbled, and threw out an arm to save himself. With a soft, crumbling sensation his hand sank into a coffin. His fingers got caught up in something like wire-wool, and he tore them away in fright. Will shone the torch on his hand, and with horror saw that it wasn't wire-wool he was holding – it was a *beard*.

Next moment he went through an agony of shaking it off. To stop himself from screaming, he examined the coffin. A yellowing label had been attached to the handle: 'Edwin Jenkinson d. 02.04.1832 – *pauper's burial, if no claimant.*'

No one had claimed him, and no one had bothered to bury him. Poor old Edwin Jenkinson had simply been left on the shelf. And here was another casket – this time from 1756!

Will shone his torch into Edwin Jenkinson's casket.

The lid had crumbled away to dust. A skeleton grinned inside. Amongst the jumbled pieces of its hand a scrap of paper read WA ORN AM.

Too intriguing to resist!

Snatching the cryptic message, with the sigh of the casket collapsing in his ears, Will made for an exit. In no time, the passages all looked the same. Reaching the end of one, he plunged down another. Dimmer and dimmer grew the light, until he began to be afraid that soon he'd be plunged into darkness. In his panic, he'd strayed far from the red-lit vaults under Nettlefold's – what if the whole street were linked by vaults, like some giant underworld?

Stop panicking. Trace the red light. Will dithered at a junction. A faint draught reached him – yes! Rushing the length of an empty passage, at last the caskets began again; they were almost friendly now. But some quality in his footfall told Will that the door at the top of the steps must have closed. Had he shut it behind him?

Heart beating, he blundered into a furry black wall. Actually bouncing off it, he stood and considered the stuffed bear. Its mild eyes looked vaguely astonished. They hadn't met, after all, since it had kindly shown him The Oddities …

Now Will knew he was shut in. Dense darkness surrounded the single light over the faded bear. He couldn't even guess where the door lay, to try it. Stories about people who'd perished because they'd strayed from the site of an air crash kept running through his thoughts. The stuffed bear was his wrecked 747, and it wasn't far from the entrance. Sooner or later Mantha would come to find him. He would stay where he was.

Poor old bear. Will shone his torch on the worn-looking pads, the dusty coat, the gnashing, faded teeth. Why did people stuff bears anyway? He supposed they were Victorian people, and that this was a Victorian bear, who'd rambled around when people wore top hats. Claws, guts, eyes, massive head, jaws, powerful legs, chest with the ghost of white markings – how would the people who shot it make something so complicated come to life? They couldn't. A bear's lifetime to make it, a moment to destroy it … Come to think of it, most of his gaming was shoot-outs …

He stayed where he was a full ten minutes thinking about the tragedy of the stuffed bear and bears and animals in general, to blot out the thought of the skeletons just three aisles away. The torch battery had faded before he noticed the knife-edges of light overhead striping the bear's chest with faint parallel lines. Light coming down through floorboards! If only he could reach them …

'Sorry about this, you old – stuffed bear.' Planting a foot determinedly on the bear's 'knee', Will hoisted himself up to face its slightly astonished expression.

'Just a bit higher, all right?' (Then he could bang under the floor – help! It's me! I'm shut in!)

The bear, called Mycroft, Will decided, had no way of telling him it *wasn't* all right, so he took the liberty of placing his knee on its shoulder. Immediately he added pressure, something happened.

With a sound like a dozen flywheels coming unstuck, the bear opened its mouth mechanically. Will watched, thunderstruck, having touched off some secret mechanism. The faded bear stretched out his neck, his glass eyes looking mildly reproving. At the end of the whirring and ticking and stretching, he burped out a little black book.

Tick – tick – tick – three seconds to pick it off the tongue! Will snatched the little book as the mouth snapped shut again. The bear looked mildly apologetic. Sorry about all that.

And what did we have here? Sliding rudely down the front of the automaton, Will shone the torch on his incredible, his amazing good luck.

'*A Receipt for the Transference of Consciousness.*'

'Receipt' was a funny word. Turned out it was probably an old word for 'recipe', or something, judging by the strangest list of ingredients that Will had ever read.

But Transference of Consciousness?

Will read on, his mind boggling, till he was sure there could be no mistake:

'*The drug will produce blurred vision and a sense*

of well-being before unconsciousness. There may be a sense of falling before the mental awareness awakens in a new host.'

There could be no doubt about it. This was Hornbeam's bodyswap cocktail. Talk about a sense of well-being. A wave of delight swept over him. Nothing could tear from him now the means to reclaim his body, his life – if he could only replicate what Horners had boiled up, one dark and secret night. It wasn't – couldn't be – beyond him, with such precise instructions, down to boiling times, under his belt. This was incredible, impossible, beyond his wildest dreams—

'Beams, you there?' Light flooded through the nearest passage with the sound of an opening door. Mantha called down the steps again. 'What are you doing down there in the dark?'

Now Will felt a bit silly. 'Nothing. I shut myself in!'

'Stop messing about, and come up – there's shedloads of stuff to do.'

A waft of fresh air led Will to the steps. Suddenly spooked by his good luck, he ran up them as if all the demons in hell were on his tail, and stood clutching his chest at the top.

He popped up beside the cold room. Since he'd been down with the skeletons, everything had changed. It was as if he'd been in another world. He had been in another world. Still, he felt triumphant with the little black book in his pocket.

'Took your time, didn't you?' Mantha swept past him with a list.

'Couldn't see where I was, could I?'

He followed her into the hall, where the unfriendly Chinese mirror showed him his shiny head.

'Handles for the Watson casket?'

Will handed over the number sixteens. Both his hands still trembled.

'Better spruce up a bit, Beamer. You can't go to Throwbones looking like a bit of old cobweb.' The grandfather clock with a chime like the knell of doom struck one thirty as though it meant it. 'That time already. We'll leave at two. Want some lunch?'

Will shook his head. He ate less than a sparrow these days.

'Got the quote for the funeral?'

Will held up two days' work. The 'Nettlefold & Dad' headed notepaper edged in black and gold carried a list of the numbers they'd been crunching since yesterday. They could submit the figures in writing to whoever inherited, at Throwbones Solicitors, at the reading of the Trice will. But they'd have to be smart today.

Mantha nodded her approval. 'I'm going up to change. Meet me in twenty. Bring down the dog coat as well.'

Once safely back in his room, Will stood the 'recipe' on his windowsill. His heart pounded as he made the calculations. Zinc oxide – they had it in the cold room, along with most of the other ingredients. The rest he could just about fudge. It was more than possible, it was – magic.

As he left the room to raid the embalming cabinets for chemicals that were not *too* unfriendly, a scrap of paper fell out of his sleeve.

He picked it up and opened it. A wisp of beard fell out. The skeleton in its casket dated 1832 seemed to grin at him once more. Of all the things that its message could have said when it had been properly unfolded and all the letters had been revealed, WA ORN AM *would* have read – wouldn't it? – in a tone of warning from his Victorian victim, from all his victims down the ages, nothing but

'BEWARE HORNBEAM'.

• ● •

It was the dog coat or nothing. All other Hornbeam attire seemed to have been pilfered for funerals. Buttoning him into it, Mantha brushed him down and stood back. 'Not too bad.' She sprayed him with Zen perfume. 'Now it doesn't niff too much.'

Crowning him with a kind of top hat, she noticed his carrier bag. 'You can't take that.'

'I can. I need a drink.'

'What is it, cranberry juice? I'll put it in my bag. Come on, hand it over.'

Reluctantly Will allowed Mantha to cram the plastic bottle, with its supremely precious contents, into her shiny black handbag.

'Take care of it, all right?'

She zipped it in. 'All right.'

It had taken him eighteen minutes and fifty-three seconds to make it. The instructions had been surprisingly simple. *First set a vessel on to boil.* He'd clicked on the kettle in his room. The rest of the mixture-making-up process were a no-brainer. Pour one thing into another. Fizz 'em up with a bit of shaking, no worries. It was the final ingredient that had set the mixture swirling and smoking, had flushed it into its tequila sunrise range of colours. The final ingredient was too strange to mention. In fact a curse would follow *immediately upon any mention of it* – this much was written in a very tiny script and underlined several times. After the pouring and fizzing and smoking had subsided there was boiling and straining. He'd used a pair of Mantha's old tights; at least he hoped they were old—

'… and it took me ages to get ready, and I couldn't find my bottle-green tights *anywhere*,' the lady in question was busy complaining. 'Haven't seen them, have you? Beams, you listening?'

'No,' said 'Beams' humbly. 'And yes.'

She did up the dog coat collar around his stringy neck. 'The buzz about the Trice inheritance has been huge. With luck Hornbeam'll be at Throwbones with the rest of Lisle Island, trying to hear the reading of the will. Then we can settle with him.'

'Settle?'

'Owes you big time, doesn't he? What's it worth not to reveal his tax position to the authorities?'

Will's pulse quickened. 'I didn't think of that.'

Mantha tapped her bag. 'Taxman's got to be interested in a few of the things in here.'

'But won't *I* get hammered for them?'

'Not if you aren't really Hornbeam. How do *you* know how much he owes?'

'But no one's going to believe—'

'Leave him to me, I know how to show that his mind isn't yours.'

No, Will thought. Leave him to me. I know how to stop his game for good. He flourished a large purple handkerchief and put up with its being arranged in his top pocket to leave a neat triangle sticking out. Mantha herself wore a delicious black suit trimmed with bottle-green velvet. A magenta streak ran through her hair and a gold snake glimmered at her throat. In shoes with heels like the snouts of crocodiles she looked, Will thought, as though she were walking on air in some jungle of the Mayas, or something …

• ● •

At Throwbones Solicitors the atmosphere was hectic. Elbowing her way through the paparazzi who had gathered for a snap of the new multi-millionaire, Mantha helped Will into a sombre-looking hall specially hired for the occasion. Buzzing with a crowd below a high table at which sat the entire Throwbones posse – with whom Nettlefold's had worked well before, as Mantha wasn't slow to point out – the room also held the picture of self-satisfaction in the plump and blooming shape of Hornbeam …

'How much is he eating?' Will squeaked. 'He's turning me into a biffa—'

'Are you on the list?' a burly attendant enquired.

'My colleague's eighty-nine, he needs a seat.' Mantha flashed her business card. 'Nettlefold & Dad, directing the Trice funeral.'

'You hope. All right. Sit here.'

At the end of the table on the platform with 'his' father and mother, Sam Levett, Mrs Rhymer and many other interested parties from the Lisle Island Hotel complex and surrounding businesses, Hornbeam gazed around the room with vast satisfaction and half a Mars bar in his mouth.

'Attention all! Can we get started?' A spaniel-like individual rose and began chocking a sheaf of papers together on a lectern.

Hornbeam swallowed and joined the ends of his pudgy fingers benevolently.

'By all means, if you're ready.'

The speaker indicated that the doors were to be closed on the flashing photographers. 'Hem, we are of course here today, this fifteenth day of October, on the occasion of—'

'Get to the point!' rapped Hornbeam.

'Hem, yes, the occasion of the reading of Mr Jonathan Bulstrode Trice's Last Will and Testament, of which the opening lines commence—'

'Never mind the opening lines. Cut to the chase!' Hornbeam again. How did he dare?

Mr Noam Throwbones, Solicitor, looked at the boy Hornbeam over his glasses. 'Of which the substantial points are, as follows: "The Lisle Island Hotel to continue to be managed by Ambergris Holdings –" '

The manager of Ambergris Holdings puffed himself at the end of the table.

' "– as will my other hotels. The fourth part of my shares to be distributed to all employees." '

A faint cheer from the floor.

'And now we come to the main business of the day. "Having no direct descendents, the substantial part of my fortune I leave in perpetuity—'

A crash splintered the silence as the photographers burst back in, and a hubbub of voices arose. It was some time before order could be re-established. Mr Noam Throwbones, Solicitor, waited gravely. At last he took up his papers again.

'What's perpetuity?' Will whispered.

'For ever,' said Mantha. 'Sssh.'

' "The substantial part of my fortune I leave in perpetuity, subject to a caveat –" '

'A what?' whispered Will.

'A special condition.'

'What's "subject to"?'

'Sssh.'

' "– a caveat reserving *a month from today for any other claimants* to step forward to have their cases examined." '

'Never mind a month, let's have the meat of it now.' Hornbeam rose, stepped forward and in a moment had ripped the Trice will from the slender hands of Noam Throwbones, Solicitor.

'Allow me.' He cleared his throat, and continued. ' "The substantial part of my fortune I leave in perpetuity to my heir-by-blood WILLIAM DANIEL DUDGEON" – all right, it says "my heirs-by-blood in the 'Lavender' line"—'

'Lavender!' Will's mother started up. 'My name before I was married!'

'Yes, that's my mother, and I'M THE HEIR – me, the flower boy at the hotel!' Hornbeam exulted. He could hardly contain himself. 'There. That's said it. Cat's out of the bag, and eating the kippers off the table. You might as well set up the accounts in my name as from now, and of course I'll be wanting the cruiser brought round to the hotel—'

'You wait your turn, Master Dudgeon!' Mrs Rhymer bopped him over the head with her umbrella, and restored the will to the executor.

'Well, well. Well, well, well, well, well. I'm afraid – I mean I'm pleased to announce that Master Dudgeon is right,' hemmed Noam Throwbones, Solicitor. 'And if no other claimant steps forward by this time in exactly a month, the substantial part of the Trice millions will indeed be transferred to his name.'

'Why wait a month?' Hornbeam rose. 'Drinks are on me at the Mitre! And so much for *you*!' he told Mrs Rhymer.

A thick silence had fallen. Then one by one photographers' cameras started flashing, and an uproar rose behind the doors as the news carried outside.

'Objection!' A tall man with a comb-over got up and waved legal papers. 'The distant family would like to object—'

'The claim has been confirmed by genetic research.' Noam Throwbones, Solicitor, cleaned his glasses wearily. 'It seems that Henry Trice had an illegitimate daughter, name of Lily Lavender—'

'That's ridiculous! This Lavender business has been inserted later!'

'Impossible. The papers were sealed.'

'But why the flower boy?'

'That is a question beyond our consideration but, as there's a condition that male descendents take precedence, William Lavender Dudgeon inherits—'

A terrific hubbub drowned out further discussion.

Parting the crowd, Hornbeam swept through the hall, his own little solicitor finning after him through the sea of photographers like a cleaner fish following a shark.

'Of all the—' Mrs Rhymer stood scandalized, looking after him.

Will gasped for breath. Mantha scooped up his frail body and carried him outside. She fanned him. 'All right?'

'I don't understand.'

'I do. He saw you – he chose you.'

'Chose me – how?'

'Never mind now.' Mantha looked grim.

'That's it. I've had it. He'll never give up my body, now he's rich in it.'

'We'll see about that.' Legs swept past them and pelted down the road. The panic infected everyone. 'They're off to the Mitre. Come on, let's get to the bar.'

• ● •

The Mitre was a lawyer's bar and restaurant.

'What's a mitre, anyway?' asked Will.

Pushing through its plush red alcoves, for once even Mantha was vague. 'Isn't it a kind of hat? There they are – watch me!'

'They' proved to be the revoltingly triumphant Hornbeam and his sidekick, the sharp little solicitor who looked like a nail file.

'Hornbeam, let me buy you a drink.' Mantha had time to wink at Will. He'd filled her in on the elixir in her bag. She'd guessed by now anyway. 'You found the recipe then. No trouble making it up?' She'd eyed him sadly. 'You know that's how Hornbeam started out?'

Will had tried to imagine Hornbeam starting out. 'When, the stone age?'

Mantha had almost started. 'Not so far wrong,' she'd said softly.

Now he saw what she was up to. If he'd been sure of his legs, he'd have joined her in 'buying' Hornbeam a pink cocktail. As it was he'd need all the strength he could get, to down a similar glassful.

Unfortunately, Hornbeam was laughing. 'Don't think you're going to get me with that one, do you?' He laughed and laughed. He was practically crying. He set down the two cocktails on a tray and raised them above his head. 'Anyone – here's a lark – drink these two drinks to swap bodies – no?'

The partygoers resumed their besieging of the bar.

'I thought not.' He turned to Mantha. 'Sorry, but there's no takers.'

His politeness was worse than the bullying. Will managed to find his mother, who was telling everyone who would listen about her son, about Lily Lavender, about how the inheritance would fund changes at the Pilchard the like of which no one could imagine, how she'd always known Will was special …

Saddened, he turned away.

The partygoers swayed in front of him, and the plush, buttoned alcoves and seating began to look like coffins ...

'Hold up, there, old man!' chaffed Hornbeam. 'You forgot the bill for the funeral.' He thrust an envelope at Will.

'How did you get this?'

'Estate solicitor.'

'But it's my own quote – these are my own figures.'

'Take care of it, *you're related.*' Hornbeam twisted his, Will's, face into a smile. The irony just got better. 'Bury Trice in a cardboard box for all I care.'

'That's exactly what we do, if it's an eco-burial,' Mantha returned crisply, joining them.

'How did you know I'd get the money – that's why you bodyswapped, isn't it?' Will persisted.

'Did the research a couple of lives ago.' Hornbeam burped loudly. 'I could see old Archie's cousin was going to have an illegitimate descendent—'

'What d'you mean, you could see?'

A roar went up as two young lawyers drained the two 'cocktails' for a bet. They swooned and writhed a bit. Everyone watched, disconcerted. Oh, well. Will guessed they'd be well confused on waking, but at least they were about the same age ...

'How did I know? Well, when married people fool about— And anyway, there's ways to see, are there not, Mantha, Mantha, Amarantha?'

'Shut up, Hornbeam.'

'Or?'

'Haven't you done enough harm for one day?'

'Still a few hours left,' burped Hornbeam, poking Will in the chest. 'And a little birdie told me you're doing so well at the dump, you won't mind staying put.'

'Dump?'

'Nettlefold's, the funeral parlour, the crash-pad for those with being-alive problems, the place of rest for those with non-heartbeat issues, the—'

'That's enough.' Will stood on his dignity. As an old man, he really thought it was his due.

'No, it's not half enough!' guffawed his revoltingly young and hearty body. He felt like pushing it in the face. 'It's not HALF enough!'

The Letter

It seemed more ridiculous by the hour. If he wasn't who he thought he was, who was he? William Lavender Dudgeon? William Daniel Trice? In any case, these were just names. But it was getting harder and harder to get a handle on who he *was*. Will lay in bed that night and felt that he was dissolving into tiny particles and drifting away into space. It gave him a feeling of spaciousness. In fact, he could get used to it.

Who was he kidding? It had been bad enough being Hornbeam.

With the news about his hidden ancestry, the story of his life to date seemed as thin as paper. Already he'd lost his body, parents, home, dog, mates, and now his identity – the identity he'd thought he had – seemed to be drifting away from him. How much more loss-making could it get?

In the still hours of a grey dawn with the dog coat hanging on the back of his bedroom door like a judge, and the sun peeping up over the pub opposite, it seemed like a topsy-turvy world he'd have to drag his old bones around in, for something like the fiftieth day.

Now Hornbeam was rich. His whole roundabout plan had fallen into place at last. No need to pretend he was a thirteen-year-old boy dependent on his parents. He could leave the Pilchard and claim the hotel as his own, lord it over Mike and Anna and anyone else he chose. Claim the entire hotel empire. Spend his life in the Caribbean, or the Maldives, if it floated his boat. Live to a ripe old age, and hop bodies again. However Hornbeam had managed to get the hotel left to himself-as-Will, he, Will, had walked right into the trap. And once he'd lain down his old bones for the last time, Hornbeam would have got away with it.

The old undertaker would leave only a coat made from the skin of a dog, a mildewed suit and a non-functioning torch. Mantha and her father would give him an eco-burial in a box. Mrs Ivy Barnes might even come and sniffle over his grave. No 'relatives' would know where he was. No one else would mourn the passing of an old man with a peculiar way of talking.

Hornbeam had thought of everything. The more Will turned it over in his mind, the cleverer he saw that it was. Dark thoughts crowded in upon him until he was left gasping for breath. Certainly it was clever. How many other unsuspecting victims would he snare in his ever-living net?

Will threw off his meagre covers and sat up. The sun rose over the pub and flooded his room with gold. Hornbeam's surroundings had been affecting him. Now his own life came flooding back. The friends he was missing spoke to him: 'Yo, Wilma, we miss you! Come back!' He visualized his football kit on the floor of his room where he'd left it the Friday before work. It was still there for all he knew. Now Saturday practice up the rec flooded back, made him rub his eyes to realize he might never play striker again. Everything, even his pencil case, his school bag, his PlayStation, suddenly seemed more vivid than anything in the boxroom at Nettlefold's …

He fell out of bed and turned the mirror round. The old gent staring back at him wouldn't fool him any more. It had been a close call. Now he realized that instead of thinking constantly about what he was missing, he'd allowed the grey stuff he'd inherited to affect his thoughts. He'd been turning into a pensioner, concerned about his aches and pains. The old grey matter had been taking over, had literally been making him lose his mind, as well as his body.

But it wasn't going to win.

Snapping Hornbeam's ancient telly on to a music channel, he cranked it up really loud. He liked 'Gatorboyz, right, and Scrugg's Rock. As well as some emo bands, he also liked drum and bass. Also he liked gaming and gaming chat rooms (where his identity was

'Paxos'), places where it was important to find out how to pick up the gun on Level Fourteen of Annihilation Road, Release Two. *And* he liked cheese dumplings and Chomps and Curly Wurlys, and playing striker with Raymond's Bay Colts, and a joke with Mum at bedtime, or maybe even a hug, when schoolwork was on his back ...

Will slammed the mirror away from him.

Why *should* Hornbeam get away with it? If he did nothing else to save himself, he could try to save other people. Taking some Nettlefold headed paper, he began to write the letter of his life to the person who'd turned his world upside down and inside out.

But as he wrote, the letter changed. He ripped it up and started again. It felt as weird as anything else had that day, to have to address it to himself:

Will Dudgeon
Pilchard Inn
Lisle Island
Raymond Bay
RB8 29R

Horners

You've had your fun at my house. Guess it doesn't feel great to have no home or parents of your own. Suppose you've been wandering around in other people's bodies for ages. I can't even imagine how long. I was going to write and threaten you with stuff Mantha and I thought out. Plus, now I know your recipe the clock's ticking.

But I've been thinking about how it feels. It must feel like no one cares about you. I'm not loving the way you've taken my body. But I guess you know I'm getting it back.

I'm asking you to stop now. Think about the kids you've dropped old bodies on. They've had a few years and then copped it, when they should have had a whole life. Some of them are down in the vaults from seventeen hundred and something. And their families never even knew they had a big fat cuckoo like you in their lives. And how did you go and treat them?

You wore out other people's bodies and dropped them like old clothes. You can't ever wipe the slate clean. But at least you can stop doing it now. Make mine the last cocktail you ever mixed. I might even let off you off lightly.

Giving you a chance to make nice here. Meet me at the Trice funeral, and we'll clink glasses after, all right? Mantha's arranging it and sending you the bill. You know it's the decent thing. You'll have a few more years as a crumbly, and then some rest. What's so bad about that? Give you the best funeral ever, when your time comes. See to it personally, I will.

Meanwhile, keep your hands off my dog and don't give my parents grief. Mantha and I have things we could do. But we don't want to do them, all right? So think about it. Think perfect rest.

Be seeing you soon, very soon.

Your latest and last swap,

WILL

What had he actually said? Will reviewed his letter. Well, he'd made a date for a meeting. Better mix up some more elixir. He'd be christening the smoking cocktail 'Bodyswap Bombshell' and delivering it personally, after his invitation. Everyone deserved a chance to change. The likelihood of Hornbeam's better instincts getting the better of him weren't great, but he had to know that Will knew that he knew the game was up—

Someone rapped on his door under the sound of Access All Hits on Channel 81.

Will folded his letter carefully and stuck it in a Nettlefold's envelope edged in black.

'KNOCK, KNOCK!' Mr Nettlefold's head appeared in a monogrammed nightcap. 'Hornbeam, are you deaf?'

'So what if I am?'

'Turn that music down!'

'My room, isn't it? No, I won't.'

The nightcap retreated before Mr Nettlefold rounded the door in a quilted purple dressing gown edged in gold. 'I'll turn it down for you.'

'Not my fault you don't like music.'

'No one in the street likes music at this time in the morning.'

'Yada, yada.' Will yawned. He didn't care a bit, he really didn't. 'Gatorboyz were cool, *any* time of day.

Mr Nettlefold pulled the plug on the telly, and the 'Gators cut out mid-riff.

'Wouldn't want any *life* in this miserable place,' Will complained bitterly. 'Might wake everyone up to having a bit of fun while they're still alive.'

'We're undertakers, we're not jumping with joy.' Mr Nettlefold regarded Will severely. 'You're taking this youthful act too far.'

'So?'

'You're acting like a spoiled teenager.'

'How would you like me to act?'

'You surprise me, Hornbeam, you really do.'

'Put this letter on the post pile, will you?'

'Who's it to?'

'That Dudgeon boy, about the Trice funeral. And shut the door on your way out.'

Mr Nettlefold turned on his heel. With great composure, he returned to remove the tasselled end of his dressing-gown cord from the door jamb.

Will thought of a number of comments he could have made. Instead he rolled around laughing for some considerable time. He had the feeling that Mr Nettlefold might have been listening.

'Are you having an identity crisis, Hornbeam?' he asked sonorously through the door. At last Will heard him walking off.

Not so much a crisis, more an identity *realignment*.

The mood had lightened, a line had been crossed. From now on, whatever he looked like, he would be himself. Cranking up Access All Hits again, infinitesimally quieter this time to show a little consideration – and anyway, wasn't he doing dullards everywhere in this neighbourhood a favour, introducing them to some good music at last? – Will put up a couple of fingers in Mr Nettlefold's general direction and felt a heap, a whole heap, better.

Ghosts

'Mantha and I have business on the other side of town this afternoon,' Mr Nettlefold had told Will after lunch. 'You'll have to hold the fort on your own – think you can do that without having a hissy-fit?'

'What's a hissy-fit?' Will had adopted his most solemn old gentleman's countenance.

'After this morning's five a.m. concert, I'm surprised you can ask.'

'Don't worry, I know what I'm doing.'

'I sincerely hope you do, Hornbeam. You've done very well up to now.'

Mantha had kissed him very lightly on the cheek – a papery cheek still burning now – had winked at him as if to say 'don't work too hard' and pulled on new midnight-blue gloves. At two fifteen precisely the door of the shop had closed behind the proprietors of Nettlefold & Dad, and the Bentley purred away to their appointments.

Silence fell over the living and the dead. The clock in the hall tolled the half-hour, and Will found himself falling asleep over the final details of the Trice funeral, to be held in just twenty-four hours' time. They'd subcontracted the Chapel of Rest side of things. Just the hearses to polish then.

For once, the phones were silent. Even the flood of journalists fishing for the time and location of the Trice memorial service had dried up. The gold-edged orders of service had been printed, flowers and bearers had been arranged, even carpeting had come under Mantha's supervision. Nothing much could cap the arrangements for tomorrow. Meanwhile, zilch was afoot on the High Street. A Wednesday half-day in the rain and, more depressingly, no one had died.

He might as well lock up shop at three. He'd give it half an hour. There was time to nip upstairs and concoct a brew. The necessary chemicals for the bodyswap elixir waited on a tray in his room. The final – and secret – ingredient for the cocktail with which Will hoped finally to persuade Hornbeam to right all his wrongs, lay in the place from which he had to pluck it. He hardly dared to think about it. What would happen when it ran out?

He climbed upstairs and put the kettle on. Breaking out a couple of key ingredients he fizzed them together and added a third, then set them reacting. He'd call back later and add the anti-reactant at just the right moment – what could go wrong?

He hobbled downstairs, cleared up the office and

snapped down the lock on the shop door. He started going upstairs to check the elixir reactions, then turned and retraced his steps as far as the office. Dialling a number from the External Services list, after accidentally ringing the dry cleaner's, he got through. 'Bob? Mr Hornbeam from Nettlefold's. Can you send your lad round to polish a couple of hearses? Tonight. By nine at the latest. Early start tomorrow – you guessed it.'

Hearses seen to. Check. He began to tidy the office again. It was while he was crossing the hall with a particularly heavy box file that he was suddenly waylaid by the dismal Chinese mirror that Mantha defended so fiercely.

Flip and flop, and other expressions of astonishment. If there wasn't something reflected in it that *wasn't present in the hall* then his name wasn't – well, it wasn't.

Will dropped his box file and the papers inside flew out and zigzagged around the hall, covering a surprising distance before they came to rest on the tiles. Dropping with a moan to his knees, he crawled up to the mirror and peered past the lacquered dragons as though he were gazing into a pool.

Mantha hadn't warned him about it. It seemed it was more than a mirror. It was like gazing into his own mind to find out that his thoughts could pierce walls and roads and distances, and even travel over the sea.

The scene was the dining room at the Lisle Island Hotel, stylish once more, and tidy. A boy and a very familiar woman bent together over a box of family photographs.

'… and here's when you were four, on that carnival float.' Will's mother pointed him out. 'Remember you were dressed as a toothbrush for that song?'

It wasn't a memory, *it was present time*. Will knew that somehow he was looking at Hornbeam, as he struggled to find the right thing to say. 'Yes, there I am.'

'Your dad lost you in the crowd, remember? We had to announce a lost toothbrush over the tannoy.'

'Why would you do that?'

'Why? Because we wanted you back.'

Hornbeam laughed like a horse. 'You wanted a giant fake toothbrush!'

'No, silly, we wanted *you*.'

Hornbeam struggled to absorb it. He took up a fresh photograph. 'Who's this?'

'Auntie Ada.'

'This?'

'Uncle Jack.'

'What about brothers and sisters?'

'You mean—'

'I haven't got any, of course.' Hornbeam let a sheaf of photos slide through his hands: beach days, picnics, birthdays, holidays … 'Family relations … I've looked for so long for a mother.'

'Why, when you've got one here?'

She pushed him and he rolled in the photographs,

getting up flushed and laughing. 'I mean, someone who likes me – loves me – for who I am.'

'And who are you?'

Hornbeam grew deadly serious. 'Your son, William Dudgeon, the Trice heir, of course.'

'Don't go back to that horrible, stiff way of talking. Not when you've been better for days.'

'I'm so tired.' He laid his head in her lap. 'So many lives … so tired …'

'Of course you are, you've not been yourself lately.'

'Someone saved me from drowning …'

'In a dream?'

'… in half a hundred lives, no one's saved me before …'

'You think you've had a past life?'

But Hornbeam had recovered himself now. 'Hasn't everyone? I expect I've been a pharaoh or something.'

Will's mother laughed. 'No one ever thinks they were a servant.'

'You wouldn't love me if you knew what I was really like.'

'Don't say things like that. You know what Doctor Stevens said.' She smoothed his hair in a sickening way. Will could hardly bear to look.

'Archie was run over,' the monster on his mother's lap murmured, after a while of being petted and smoothed.

'Archie?'

'Trice. Knocked down on a corner in London. Good thing he'd fixed up his will. Cousin Henry got everything. Henry was old. His son, Jonathan, was sickly. So I – Archie, knew he'd have to wait.'

'Wait? What for?'

'For a great-great-grandson – like me – to inherit!'

'Did you see her?' Will's mother's hands winnowed the pile of brown photographs. 'Lily Lavender, my grandmother.'

She had steady, dark eyes and a serious expression under a halo of light hair and lace. Hornbeam nodded, and studied 'his' ancestress carefully. 'Archie knew Henry had a secret daughter. He made a condition in his will so his fortune could come down through her.'

'How do you know all this?' Will's mother asked, laughing and puzzled.

'Researched it online, didn't I?' Hornbeam improvised.

She began to sketch a simple family tree in the margins of a magazine. 'Archie, his cousin Henry – *his* son, Jonathan Trice, who's just died; Lily, Jonathan's secret older sister, my grandmother. Jonathan has no children so now you're first in the male line of descent. Who'd have thought you'd turn out to be a millionaire?'

Hornbeam turned radiant eyes up to her. 'Who'd have thought?'

Bare-faced or what, when he'd fixed it somehow. Will turned away in disgust.

'You've been better since the will reading though, haven't you?' his mother coaxed.

'A little better,' Hornbeam admitted.

Do me a favour.

'You've stopped feeling so mixed up?'

'A hundred and forty million straightens a lot of things out.'

'Yes, I suppose it does. What would you like to do tomorrow?'

'Nothing, until the funeral's over,' Hornbeam said virtuously.

'Well, that won't be long now.'

Will couldn't believe these two. Where was his dad?

The scene in the mirror fuzzed and shifted. For some reason, his father was chopping wood on Archie's patio. A stack of logs waited beside him. He chopped and chopped and chopped, disregarding chips of wood flying off, and throwing down piles of firewood. Will felt as though he was viewing the scene through the wrong end of a telescope.

'Dad?' he called. 'I'm coming back! Don't be angry!'

His father froze and looked up. Seagulls beat on the wind, with their keening cries bridging the gulf between them.

'Where are you?' The hatchet fell from his grasp; his father searched the air, unseeingly. 'Will, are you there?'

'Hornbeam! What's going on?'

The cold-room door opened suddenly, and footfalls whistled past his face. Will watched from his position on the floor beside the Chinese mirror as Mantha's feet became glued to the stairs by a pink sludge frothing down them.

'Get him up!' ordered Mr Nettlefold.

Hands jerked him upright and set him on his feet.

'We've been rattling the shop door for ten minutes. What on earth were you doing on the floor?' Mr Nettlefold's eyes drilled through his brain.

'Mirror needed polishing, did it, Hornbeam?' Mantha helped him out.

'Thash it.' Will adjusted his teeth.

'What's this stuff on the stairs?'

Will tottered over and scratched his head. Mantha skipped up to his room on a hunch and reappeared in moments. 'It's just a chemical reaction.'

'A chemical reaction?' Mr Nettlefold's face darkened. 'I don't expect to come home to find a *chemical reaction* on the stairs, and the only responsible person on the premises lying in front of a mirror.'

'Give him a break, he passed out.' Mantha put an arm around him. 'Come on, Beams, mind your feet.' Guiding him upstairs, she put him to bed while clearing the room of a standing trail of foam. 'How long did you leave it without the anti-catalyst?'

Will shrugged speechlessly. It was as though the person who'd set the bodyswap elixir going had done it in another universe.

'You can't go on like this, you're getting careless. Anyway, I bought you a suit for the big day tomorrow. We'll attend the end of the service, then go straight to the wake.' She shook out a small but perfect dark suit on to his bed. 'It'll be great for the conference as well – you haven't forgotten the conference?'

'Think about it day and night.'

'Want some dinner on a tray later?'

Will grunted.

'I'll mash it up, don't worry. Bearers confirmed?'

Will grunted again.

'Hearses?'

'Being cleaned tonight.'

'I know you've got a lot on your mind.' She paused at the door as if she had the merest inkling of an idea how much. 'I told you not to mess with that mirror. Get some sleep if you can, we've got a big day tomorrow.'

Archie RIP

The Trice funeral had been the most magnificent day for the firm of Nettlefold & Dad since records had begun. Hornbeam had been forced to sign the cheques, and the estate had spared no expense.

Jonathan B. Trice had enjoyed the most expensive casket that the firm was capable of sourcing. With solid brass handles and a lining of silk, it had been smothered with lilies and lavender in honour of the new heir's great-grandmother, Jonathan's secret sister.

'He'd only known about her since opening the special condition of Archie's will, when he came to make his own,' Noam Throwbones, Solicitor, explained with dignity over a mini sausage roll.

The hotel magnate had been borne to his last resting place with great solemnity, followed by a cast of film stars, artists and writers, who turned up at the discreet memorial service as though they'd been magicked from some secret existence only Jonathan knew about.

Mantha showed Will the autographs she'd gathered in her violet-scented book.

'Rafe Nialls, he's been in that desert plane-crash thing – and Roma Vale, she's been in loads of stuff—'

'What about that bloke from *Hellboy 3*?'

'Why would I bother with *him*?' Mantha tossed her head.

Fountains stacked with tinkling champagne glasses greeted their return to the hotel, where marquees had been set out on the lawn.

Mr Nettlefold had been beside himself with self-importance, and had been as happy as a funeral director could get. Tucking a napkin into his shirt, he'd settled for an enormous plate of food at the wake, or party for friends and relatives, to which undertakers weren't usually invited.

'But thish is speshial, after all,' he told Will over his fourth drink. Will felt mildly revolted. He wasn't used to seeing the usually reserved and elegant Mr Nettlefold in a somewhat silly light. 'Went off smooth as silk, didn't it? Good old Hornbeam, bringing in businesh left, right and centre.'

'Yeah,' Will said. 'Whatever.'

He glimpsed the young heir in his pin-striped glory of a suit over the heads of distant relatives and hangers-on. He felt sick as he realized he was entirely unarmed, and unable to fulfil any of the threats or promises he'd made in his letter.

Now the young heir was embracing him. 'Mr Hornbeam! Tried the chocolate fountain?'

'Just call me Will, all right?'

'If you'll call me will *benefactor*, and heir to millions, ha, ha!' gloated Hornbeam. 'Thanks for the letter. Nice proposal – not.'

He was talking more like a teenage boy with every passing hour as Will's own youthful genes began to take over his, Hornbeam's, mind. In a reverse process to the one Will had recently detected within himself, Hornbeam was morphing into his assumed identity. Soon the change would be irreversible. Fact is, it was already.

The fact was that the foam-down-the-stairs incident had had an unexpected sequel. When he'd gone to fetch more secret ingredient for a fresh batch of elixir, the larder had been empty and the pantry bare – quite literally his chance had dried up. Bitterly Will realized he'd wasted the last opportunity he was going to get to concoct the 'Bodyswap Bombshell' cocktail he'd been banking on toasting Hornbeam with, in the bar where the nightmare had begun …

'You don't have to worry,' he said. 'I'm trapped in this body now.'

'Don't take it so hard, old man,' beamed the young heir. 'I'm in a good mood. What would you like? Anything you want – flying lessons, trip to Monte Carlo – what about Buenos Aires—'

'Stay away from my mum and dad, all right?'

'I'm retiring them to Bournemouth anyway.'

Will saw his mum and dad now over the heads of the crowd, playing mine hosts for all they were worth. 'Bournemouth?'

'Why not? Place for crumblies, isn't it? Besides, I've got plans for the Pilchard ...'

'Where's my dog?'

'Wherever you left him.'

'That's not funny.'

'I never said it was.' The young millionaire spotted a film star, and swept off to amuse his guests.

• ● •

The merriment began to disgust him. Will wandered off through the hotel. The burble and buzz of the guests downstairs faded, and he was alone with Archie's vision of elegance, his clean-cut lounges with deco motifs on the walls, mirror-tiled bathrooms and stunning views out to sea. Respecting the style of the hotel, Jonathan had changed very little.

But what was this?

On the private beach below, the makings of a burger bar had been erected. Much of the patio had been covered in a ball pool and snooker tables, with a popcorn machine in pride of place. On the floating diving platform in Archie's hidden cove a full jazz orchestra tuned up for the entertainment that evening. Synchronized swimmers in green and orange hats practised making patterns under ultraviolet lights. Archie would have approved. But a hoarding announcing that Ambergris Holdings invited new shareholders to Realize the Commercial Potential of the Hotel over a picture of a new block of flats, made the evening feel like the last bubble in a dream that would shortly burst.

As if it mattered to him. Hauling his old bones down a service stair, Will finally reached a concrete well at the bottom, in which was set a single door. Since being old, he hated lifts. They brought him out in a sweat of claustrophobia, even though his habit of taking the stairs brought him to the verge of a heart attack.

And now he would have to go up again.

It was a part of the hotel complex he'd never found himself in before. On the off-chance of an exit to the first floor, he tried the fire door in the stained concrete wall. Usually he'd have jumped into the lift without a second thought – service stairs weren't usually a part of his breezy, uncomplicated young world. And this stairwell was especially tucked away, the webs that coated its corners waving in a draught coming in around *a second door concealed behind the first.*

Will tried the handle. It opened to a blast of cool air, and lights flickered on overhead. A private cinema revealed itself, complete with plush seats and curtain. A series of clicks announced the opening of a speech from a recorded voice: 'Please take a seat. I'll be with you in a moment.'

Glad to take the weight off his feet, Will chose a seat at the front. The moment he sat down the lights dimmed, and the curtain swept back with a flourish. The whirr of a projector introduced a countdown onscreen. Five ... four ... three ... Will felt a thrill of anticipation – what would he see? ... two ... one ...

Archie!

'THIS IS WHAT I USED TO LOOK LIKE,' boomed the same mournful voice that had invited him to sit down, over a famous picture of Archie onscreen. His hair was slicked down and parted in the middle, his neck choked in a stiff white shirt collar under a tweed jacket. He looked part playboy, part car salesman.

'THIS IS WHAT I LOOK LIKE NOW.' Young Archie was replaced by a very old man with a domed forehead and whiskers, speaking to camera. 'Yes, this is me, Archibald Naylor Trice,' the old man continued, joining his trembling hands together in front of him. 'But it's not me, in my body. I want to put on record that my life has been stolen by this man.'

A still photograph of the same old man appeared. Confusing.

The speaking old man resumed. 'This man, who of course looks like me, invited me for a whisky at my club. I was twenty-three years old at the time, and in my prime. Remember, I looked like this.'

The picture of Archie again.

'When I woke up next morning, I looked like this.'

The speaking old man held up a hand like a claw. 'He put something in the whisky. I felt his mind taking over mine before I fell asleep that night. I'd been tricked into drinking some secret mixture – good God, I'll never know what! – that had enabled this man's mentality to take control of my body, and leave my mind, in turn, in his decrepit frame. You see what I inherited – these withered arms and legs. He has lived my life for ten years, and now my life draws to a close. He spends little time here, except for his parties, and has yet to find this film, which I leave to posterity as a warning. HAVE NOTHING TO DO WITH THIS MAN!'

A picture of Archie again filled the screen. This time his neat black moustache looked sinister, and *Hornbeam beamed from his eyes*. Will grasped the seat and the cinema spun around him as the warning boomed out again and again – HAVE NOTHING TO DO WITH THIS MAN, HAVE NOTHING – HAVE NOTHING HAVE NOTHING HAVE NOTHING TO DO WITH THIS MAN …

• • •

Mrs Rhymer's kitchen was a place Will had always been afraid of. With its vaulted ceiling hardly visible above a vast collection of copper pans and implements, it had always seemed mysterious and threatening, and Mrs Rhymer herself didn't help.

Now it seemed like a place of refuge. Hobbling down

service corridors until he thought he'd collapse, at last Will spotted an easy chair in a distant rectangle of light. Never mind that it was in the lair of that denizen of the kitchen underworld, Mrs Rhymer. He had to sit down, or die.

'Well, don't mind me, I'm sure!' The housekeeper herself paused in the act of sharpening a knife.

Will collapsed like a sack of potatoes on what was surely her chair. The light was so dim he was sure she'd carve her fingers instead of the chicken in front of her.

'Archie Trice,' he panted. 'Swapped!'

'What about him? And by the way, the party's upstairs.'

'See, Hornbeam-as-Archie … he must have left a condition in his will … so he could find him – me – leave the hotel to himself and be rich again!'

'Pass me that plate, since you're sitting on it.'

Will passed her a very large white oval plate with some difficulty. Mrs Rhymer immediately began arranging slices of chicken on it, ending with the legs and wings. Without pausing, she stripped another chicken of its limbs and began slicing again. A line of birds ahead of her on the scrubbed kitchen table awaited the same treatment.

Footsteps approached. Will took to the floor behind his chair.

'Mr Lavender Trice says where's the burgers?' Will peeped round his chair.

Unbelievable! The henchmen Hornbeam had recruited were from among the very worst slime at school – Gareth Chambers, for starters.

'In the oven,' said Mrs Rhymer sourly, about to give him away, Will could see.

'Get them out on the table,' ordered Gareth Chambers.

'Get them out yourself.'

'Mr Lavender Trice said he'd come down himself if there was any trouble.'

'He can come down all he wants, they won't be any quicker.' Mrs Rhymer set her jaw and basted something in the oven that sent out acrid smoke.

Emerging as soon as the coast was clear, Will copped the flak from this encounter as Mrs Rhymer's carving entered a vicious phase. 'Nasty – little – so-and-so – thinks he – owns the – *world*.' Tearing the wings from a fourth roasted chicken she slammed the oven door with her foot. 'Come down here and – throw your – *weight* around, will you?' Legs off, knife in fresh breast. 'Not in my kitchen, I tell you – no jumped-up flower boy telling *me* what to do—'

And suddenly there was the jumped-up flower boy himself – Hornbeam, in a perfect Eton collar and a tweed suit, like Archie's, telling her what to do. 'Get the sausages up there, will you? And put on a load more chips. You – old man,' Hornbeam added, choosing not to recognize Will. 'Get these chicken platters upstairs, now.'

Will humbly loaded himself with plates, and paused to arrange them along his arm at the door.

'I got Bartleby's sausages; they take a bit longer, but they're good,' Mrs Rhymer was saying.

'I don't care what they're like, get them up there,' Hornbeam repeated.

'I don't send out things that aren't cooked.'

'Send them up, I tell you, you stupid old woman!'

'Watch your tongue in my kitchen, if you don't mind.'

'Rhymer, you're dismissed!'

'You aren't officially the owner until the month's up, so you can't dismiss anyone.'

'Yet. Where does that leave you when I can?'

Mrs Rhymer put her hands on her hips. 'I hope someone else turns up and claims the money – that'll take a stuck-up little pub hand like you down a peg. Who d'you think you are in that monkey-suit, Toad of Toad Hall?'

'The party this evening is nineteen-twenties fancy dress.'

'You, as Archie Trice?'

'I *was* Archie Trice, you old dingbat.'

'He had more class in his little finger.'

They faced one another furiously. Suddenly Hornbeam tore down a rack of ladles, which sprang all over the floor. Mrs Rhymer snorted like a horse. Unhooking a copper pan, she bonged Hornbeam over the head with it. Hornbeam staggered, and took up a fire-iron. In front of the roaring range they struggled, casting monstrous shadows on the wall. Will watched, horrified – two combatants of equal strength locking horns with an endless number of sharp implements within reach, both with a proper desire to give one another a savaging …

Suddenly he didn't care what came of it. He turned on his heel and walked out into a small sitting room. They could wrangle for hours, fall in the fire and end up spitted like pigs for all he cared …

What was he saying? *This was his body!*

Throwing his chicken platters on to a settee, he limped back to the heated nether regions of the kitchen, where bangs and clatters still reverberated. As Will re-entered the kitchen, Hornbeam was fielding coals with a frying pan. Mrs Rhymer hurled the coal bucket. He caught it, and winded her with it. Closing, they fell on one another.

Finding the nearest thing to hand to separate them and to protect Hornbeam's borrowed body from further injury at the hands of the Rhymer hell-being, Will tottered up with a giant jelly and heaved it all over them.

The effect was instantaneous.

'The jelly!' Mrs Rhymer took in the enormity of it. 'The jelly shaped like the hotel!'

'What's he done with it?' Hornbeam wailed. 'What's this in my collar?'

'He's ruined it, that's what he's done!'

'Well,' Will scolded, 'it's your own fault.'

They stood there with a half a quivering hotel on their backs.

'And I don't want any more of it,' Will finished severely. 'The fighting, I mean. I'm going now.'

'Keep still, I can save the tower,' Hornbeam was saying as he left.

'You've got the east wing on your shoulder.'

'*Still*, I said.'

'Still, yourself.'

• ● •

The synchronized swimmers' hats arranged themselves into flowers under the ultraviolet lights, and melted into ever more complicated patterns. The floating jazz band finished a number with a flourish, and the watching diners applauded. A few of them were of the opinion that a rocket needed to be put under the polite amusements on offer. Finishing burgers, the Gareth Chambers posse bombed into the water from the rocks. A shockwave ran round the patio. The wake had officially ended and the evening's entertainment had well and truly begun.

'LISLE ISLAND HOTEL WELCOMES WILLIAM LAVENDER TRICE,' read the banners. 'A NEW ERA BEGINS!'

Will wandered like a stranger through the party, sometimes seeing Mantha in freeze-frame, laughing over a drink; sometimes glimpsing his parents. He felt as though he were walking through The Oddities, the ghosts of all those down the ages who had been bodyknapped by Hornbeam. All at once he caught up with his mum. She turned and flashed him a brilliant smile, which made him feel like blubbing.

'Pleased to meet you, and you are …?'

'The undertaker.'

'You're not too tired, I hope?'

Will staggered.

'Sit down – you must be exhausted. What a send-off the old man had, didn't he?'

'The Jonathan Trice funeral's probably the biggest we'll ever do,' Will agreed, taking a seat overlooking a dais on which stood the boy-wonder, Hornbeam, tapping a microphone.

'And now my son inherits. Look at him up there,' Will's mother sighed. 'He hasn't been himself at all lately. I do hope the money won't affect him too much. Apparently Jonathan was very unhappy. So many rich men are.'

Will considered this. 'He's thirteen years old with his whole life in front of him, and he's got a hundred and forty million pounds. Think I could handle it,' he said.

'With money comes responsibility. Archie Trice died because of it.'

Will looked at her. 'How?'

'Worried out of his mind over his stocks and shares

apparently – stepped out into the street, and was knocked down by a cab. Died in hospital.'

Not before Hornbeam had skipped bodies, somehow, to some poor nurse or doctor, Will noted – or perhaps to a patient in the next bed. What couldn't he have done, with a phial of the elixir in his pocket? Will had never thought about this before. Quick mental arithmetic told him that the old bodysnatcher could have skipped straight from the dying Archie to the body *which had become the old Hornbeam* ...

'James Hornbeam, Sailor,' he murmured.

'I'm sorry?'

'Something I saw in The Oddities. A book I'm reading.'

'We consulted a lot of old books over family history,' his mother said conversationally. 'Archie made his fortune in corsetry, then when flappers came the fashion changed, and no one wanted corsets any more. Jonathan's investments saved the day. We've found out all sorts of things. Sure you're comfortable there? I can fetch you a rug.'

'I'm comfortable,' Will said. 'Where's Da— Mr Dudgeon?'

She looked away. 'Mr Dudgeon's upset. He's found out we're moving to Bournemouth, and the fact is – we don't want to go.'

'So why do you have to?'

'Oh, well, we do what we're told by the estate.

We don't want to upset anybody. William – we call him Mr William now – wants us to be gone by next Monday.'

'FRIENDS,' the microphone boomed. 'Friends, I'd like to welcome you here to a new era of wonderful luxury at the Lavender chain of hotels! Please take the opportunity to enjoy the entertainment on offer. I need hardly tell you that in the next month or two, everything will change. Developing the golf course with timeshares and luxury flats will—'

'Ruin the island!' someone shouted.

'Take that member of staff outside.' Hornbeam waited while a fracas developed in the crowd and someone was taken out, protesting. He plastered on a smile and continued. 'In the tradition of my ancestor the great Archie Trice, a prize will be awarded to the first person to swim to the buoy and back in fancy costume! Last one in's a ninny!'

Will applauded Hornbeam's speech with mounting rage as a collection of pierrots, gangsters and Charlie Chaplins rushed past him to take to the water. Marked with a flashing light, the buoy bobbed some distance beyond the diving platform. It would be a strong swimmer who reached it and returned in the dark, weighed down by fancy dress.

His mother took out a handkerchief. 'Of course, we'll only be in the way, in the hotel now that William's – Mr William's – got so many plans. But he's demolishing the

Pilchard as well, and we *were* rather fond of the place, and he's gutted his bedroom, already—'

Will had heard enough. 'I hear Bournemouth's quite nice,' he said. 'I'm sure you're going to enjoy it.'

He turned on his heel and went back through the bar, his heart breaking. 'Set me up a whisky. A big one.'

'Sure you want a double, granddad?' asked Mike, the barman, who he'd used to back Arsenal with.

'Set it up. A double.'

If he'd never had a whisky in his life before, now was the time to start. But when the drink was served, he felt sick. It tasted like smoke-flavoured vomit. Pushing it away, he swept through reception. There stood the statue of the silver flapper, the dancer he was so fond of. The thin black line circling her slender silver neck, where her head had been stuck on again, only made her seem more fragile. As he passed the desk, he slipped her into an inside pocket. He would have something for himself from tonight, at least, even if he'd lost everything else.

Stepping out through the lounge door some time later, he cooled off overlooking the dark bay. Beyond the rocky outcrop hiding the cove, the sea tractor would be busy ferrying partygoers back to the mainland. Cheers went up now and again over the sound of the band, he assumed marking the return of swimmers. He had no idea where Mantha was, whether the grey Bentley had swept her away without collecting him or not. Frankly, he didn't care. Whether he stayed or went home to his miserable boxroom at Nettlefold's, this felt like the last night of his life, the last night like this he ever wanted, at least. He *had* no home. No life. No hope. No—

What was that lump on the rocks? Will's heart began to hammer.

Scrambling with extreme slowness and caution along the rocky arm that protected the swimming cove from the open sea, he at last reached a body. To the last moment, he thought it was a seal. Only when he heaped away the seaweed did his own features show whitely under the moon.

Clapping his withered lips on to the purple mouth, he breathed life back into his own body.

Hornbeam coughed and retched. 'There's no need for that.'

Will clapped him on the back.

Hornbeam looked up. 'You saved me…again.'

Compassion overwhelmed Will's darker thoughts. 'Resting after your swim to the buoy, weren't you?'

'I've almost … drowned your body. Not a very … good tenant of it, am I? That is, of course, why you care …'

'I never wanted you to die.'

'Because I'd … damage your body,' Hornbeam repeated.

'Not altogether.' Will thought about it. 'You can't be all bad. Mantha likes you.'

'I'm touched.'

'Human being, aren't you?'

'I was … once,' said Hornbeam, convulsing.

'Lie back, you'll be all right in a minute.' Will waited, and the sea swashed on the rocks, and someone cheered on the other side of the cliff, and the jazz band played crazily on. Fireworks arced over the bay. Good thing he hadn't had to call for help. No one would have heard him. 'How come you're so far off course?'

'Got washed round the rocks. Haven't swum in eighty years. 'Fraid I'm out of practice.'

'Not surprised.' Will waited some more. The lights of the hotel winked beyond the long arm of the rocks. 'How will we get you home?'

'Home.' Hornbeam laughed hollowly, and coughed.

He might have to call for help, yet. In the meantime he cradled Hornbeam's head in his hands, and felt his own heavy hair. 'Don't try to talk if you don't want to.'

'Thought I could make the buoy. I'm not as strong as I thought.'

'You mean, *I'm* not.'

'Think I've … ruined … your body. Not used to being young. Thought I was as strong as a … mountain.'

Knocks and scrapes were rampant, all right. Will examined the throat and head. A huge bruise from being bonged by Mrs Rhymer with a copper pan and various other biffs and scratches blighted the forehead of the young millionaire.

'Dive with me now. Take it back.' The hands, his own hands, grasped the front of his jacket.

'You're mad.' Will struggled to disengage himself.

'You saved me … didn't have to …'

'What anyone would've done.'

The hands became desperate, clutching at him. 'The one *good* thing I can do in … half a hundred lives … please … I beg you … don't stop me …'

With an enormous effort, the body seemed to raise itself like Frankenstein's monster. Wrapping its arms around the decrepit Will, it toppled into the water, dragging him with it into the stunning cold and darkness of the ocean, squeezing the life and breath from his fragile old body and dragging him, like a dead weight, to the bottom.

The Nettlefold Award

'... and he wasn't the only one almost drowned at that party last night,' Will's mother's voice was saying. 'Paper says an old man was found, stolen statue in his pocket dragged him down like a stone ... taken to hospital unconscious ... when they went to find him, he'd gone missing ...'

Seashells clinked to and fro across the sea floor like chains being dragged by the waves, curling overhead like creamy sheets being turned back in order for him to sleep, sleep ...

Will woke from a dream of drowning. A couple of familiar voices whispered quietly somewhere near him, a medical smell seemed to be everywhere, and his body was full of twitches.

'... we're just lucky someone spotted Will—'

'Mr William.'

'You can't go on calling him "Mr William", he's your son.'

'Don't want to upset him, do we? He isn't conscious, yet I suppose, but ...'

'Of course he's conscious, he's dozing. No permanent damage, they said.'

Will raised his head very slightly. A familiar-looking boy of thirteen looked back at him from the full-length mirror opposite his hospital bed. The boy had tubes running into his arm. He had a bruise on his head, and matted hair. His beloved parents sat beside him, lucky dog that he was.

Will grinned. William Daniel Dudgeon grinned back. O joy of being gloriously back in his own body, who knew or cared how! Delight flooded in with the knowledge. His toes reach the end of the bed! His arms and hands responded strongly when twitched! His legs had thick muscles; his mouth a full set of teeth! Will raised his arm and found it young, smooth and strong. 'William Daniel Dudgeon,' he said loudly, to test his voice. He felt like springing out of bed and running down the corridor, shouting. Instead, he turned to the 'rents. 'Mum – Dad – good to see you!'

'Oh, Will – William.' His mother's face loomed beside him.

'Stay calm, Will, you're on a drip. You were found on the rocks; they're re-hydrating you, so keep still.'

He could see the tube disappearing into his arm, beside his father's reassuring hand. 'Dad – the old man in the paper—'

'Don't tire yourself.'

'I'm not tired. I feel great.'

'What old man?'

'The one who almost got drowned because of the statue in his pocket – where is he now?'

His father checked the paper. 'They think in Romania.'

'Romania?'

'An air ticket booked in his name, or something – don't try to sit up.'

'William – Mr William – shall I get you a drink?'

'Will, Mum, don't be silly. And by the way, I'm cancelling all redevelopment and demolition plans on the island – and what date is it?'

'The sixteenth.'

'No way.' He sprang out of bed and an alarm beeped on the monitor overhead.

A nurse appeared. 'Need hooking up again?'

Good-humouredly, she reattached him to his tube. It gave him time to think, at least. The dream of drowning had been real. How had Hornbeam been able to find it in his crabbed old heart to sacrifice himself?

Hornbeam had drawn them both into the water. Exhausted, and with the weight of the statue in Will's pocket, they'd sunk together like stones.

It was a bold – a brave – move.

Hornbeam had gambled on his aged former body being half drowned before the young one he now inhabited was. Once he, Will, was unconscious, and his decrepit frame was temporarily vacant *Hornbeam must have voluntarily taken up residence again* – and there would have been nowhere for Will's consciousness to go, but back to his own youthful body …

Will remembered the tender scene, viewed in the mirror, of his mother smoothing Hornbeam's head. Perhaps some stirrings of conscience had led him to give her son back to her again. It was impossible to say what had—

'He's looking pretty sparky. We'll discharge him tonight,' the nurse said.

'Before midday – I can't stay here.'

'Will,' objected his mother.

'I've got to *be* somewhere,' Will pleaded.

• ● •

The somewhere was Throwbones Solicitors. It was the last day of the month reserved for any other claimants to step forward before William Lavender Dudgeon officially inherited the Trice fortune. No one else had stepped forward so far. At twelve noon the time would be up. It was only a formality now – a matter of signing several documents. In his dreary front office Noam Throwbones laid out the pens. He straightened the chairs and wound the clock and shut its glass case with precision. They were leaving it rather late. Well, they would soon be here …

Will's parents had understood that, as long as he felt up to it, it was important to appear before twelve to sign the papers confirming his inheritance. Otherwise they would ring Throwbones Solicitors and have the papers sent over by courier. But Will had been out of bed already. A scan had revealed no damage, discharge papers were signed and in moments he was shivering in the hospital car park while his father reversed the car.

But an accident on Rendelsham High Street had blocked access to the bypass. Will's dad fumed a little. But Will made a joke of it – how could they not laugh when the world was young and coloured thirteen, and strength and happiness sang in his veins? He'd get out and push the car! And laugh like a madman while he did it!

'You're in a good mood,' his father joked. 'You should half drown more often.'

'David.' Will's mother looked ashen. 'What a dreadful thing to say.'

'Get on, will you, some people are in a hurry!' Will's father honked his horn impatiently, getting a bit pink round the gills.

'Lighten up,' Will said. 'We're all in the same boat.'

'You're mellow after getting out of hospital.'

'David.'

'Well, you must admit, it's a change.'

At last they were flagged past the accident. 'Look at that – old man's stepped off the pavement. Looks a bit shattered, doesn't he?' Mrs Dudgeon noticed.

Will's head whipped round as they passed. The top of

the head, the hoary hair, the familiar suit Mantha had bought him – the eyes had met his, had sent a thrill of horror coursing through his newly reclaimed body as its previous tenant stood confused and bloodstained on the kerb.

At eleven fifty-three precisely, Will entered the fusty office. Noam Throwbones, Solicitor, rose with an audible creak and bid them 'Good morning' with the people-greeting skills of a wardrobe.

'Sorry we're late,' Will's father apologized. 'Old man got knocked down in the High Street, traffic was backed up as far as—'

'No other claimant has presented themselves before the requisite time of twelve noon,' interrupted the solicitor, glancing at the clock. 'Could you sign here – and here – confirming your right to the inheritance.' Noam Throwbones offered Will a pen and pointed out the sections to be signed. 'Mr Shingles here is a witness.'

Mr Shingles was Hornbeam's solicitor, who'd finned along in his wake at the will reading a month ago.

'Such a mad dash,' said Will's mother, taking off her coat.

'Nettlefold & Dad are making a presentation at the Funeral Directors' Conference this morning,' Will said, draping his mother's coat on her chair, and not in any hurry to confirm his inheritance. 'And Mantha – Amaranth Nettlefold – is scheduled at midday. Her speech is on 'A Green Way Downward', that's six feet down, under a cowpat—'

'Such a funny name, but they made a good job of the funeral,' said Will's mother. 'She really is an unusual person.'

'Also please initial here – and here.' Noam Throwbones's finger tapped more sections for Will to sign.

'Better read it.'

'No need for that.'

Will read it out anyway: 'I hereby state that I, William Lavender Trice, do hereby renounce my former name and parents—'

He looked around. His parents both had signs of grey hairs. His heart went out to both of them. How lucky he was to have them. His mind expanded, flitted over the rooftops to the Rendelsham Millennium Hall. It entered the auditorium, where Mantha's PowerPoint presentation had entered its Moral High Ground phase. *We believe in eco-burials and in avoiding the environmentally unfriendly embalming process, even if Uncle Rodney has to spend the night in a freezer.* They'd run over the speech so many times. He could practically hear her. *We're not here for very long. Our lives pass like a flash of lightning. We at Nettlefold & Dad believe in doing the right thing …*

'Please,' said Noam Throwbones.

The clock stood at three minutes to twelve.

'Talking of renouncing things,' Will set down his pen. 'I've got an announcement to make.'

• • •

Will entered the auditorium in a hurry, as the conference was closing. It was his great good luck to be in time to catch the tail-end of her presentation; shutting down the PowerPoint window at the lectern, Amaranth Nettlefold glanced up and saw him, curled her lip and continued leading up to the presentation of a cup.

'... and finally, in setting up the Nettlefold Award for Excellence in Green Burials, I'd like to acknowledge the part that my assistant, James Hornbeam, has played in helping me with the idea. He can't be with us today, and has unfortunately gone missing ...'

A hum ran round the auditorium.

'... but every effort is being made to locate him, and I know that the Guild of Funeral Directors would want me to give him their congratulations. And now it's my pleasure to make the first presentation of The Nettlefold Award for responsible practice to—'

'Wait!' commanded Will, walking the length of the maroon carpet to the lectern through the centre of all the VIPs in the funeral world as though parting the Red Sea. 'I'll add a five-thousand-pound purse to that!'

A buzz of excitement ran round the auditorium.

The young Trice heir! In recognition of his ancestor's magnificent funeral! How generous!

'In memory of Archie and Jonathan Trice,' Will added, 'and with your agreement,' he acknowledged Mantha, 'maybe this award could be called the Trice–Nettlefold Cup?'

'Very generous. Nettlefold–Trice,' Mantha corrected. 'And now I'd like to ask the firm of Tremorrow and Son to accept this cup and purse – thank you!'

Huge applause. The young Tremorrow, shiny with embarrassment, sprang up to take the trophy. He waved it and ran up the aisle as the hall rocked with congratulations. Who would have thought that a bunch of undertakers could be half so lively?

'Had a knock on the head, or something?'

'Sorry?'

'Giving away money – what brought that on?' Mantha regarded Will sourly.

She didn't know he had his body back!

'You don't understand, I'm not—'

Before he could make her hear him, a tide of joyful funeral directors whisked her away to make a statement to the local press. Will watched her extraordinary hat –or 'fascinator', as she'd told him it was called: a bit of felt and net gripped to the side of the head, this one in the shape of a spider – disappear into the crowd.

'Not bad, eh?' Mr Nettlefold was positively aglow.

'And your very generous gesture has raised the profile of the award considerably.'

'Last thing I'll be able to give away,' Will said cheerfully. 'I'm skint.'

Mr Nettlefold laughed in a very ingratiating way, showing all his teeth.

'No, really,' said Will. 'I gave it all away.'

'*All* away? Surely—'

'Just now. At Throwbones.'

Mr Nettlefold regarded the young millionaire seriously. He seemed to be dressed in the rags of some tweed costume …

'And don't complain about people playing their music loudly in future, or I'll cancel your account with the estate.'

Mr Nettlefold started. 'I wouldn't dream of it.'

'A friend of mine told me that you told him off for playing his music too loud.'

'At five thirty in the morning. Surely he didn't mention that.'

'Oh, he'd thought about that.'

'How can you know?'

'You get to know a lot of things when you just signed away a hundred and forty million.'

'You signed it away.' At last Mr Nettlefold began to pay attention. 'You can't have – but why?'

Will recalled the scene of less than an hour ago. His announcement had certainly made everyone sit up.

'Talking of renouncing things …' He'd actually jumped on to old Throwbones's desk, had actually stopped the fusty old office clock with the thump, had tapped the top of Noam Throwbones's head with a pencil, for everyone's attention. He could see their faces now. 'I RENOUNCE MY PART IN THE TRICE MILLIONS NOW AND FOR EVER –'

'What?' His mother looked nonplussed.

'You can't!' his father exclaimed.

'Think!' Noam Throwbones wrung his hands.

'– NOW AND FOR EVER, with three conditions. One, the money's to be made over to a new organization called the Lisle Island Wildlife Trust for the benefit of all the seals and birds, and no new building to be allowed, ever. Two, there's to be five hundred pounds a year set aside for flower boys at the Lisle Island Hotel, for *ever*—'

'In perpetuity,' noted Noam Throwbones, shaking his head.

'In perpetuity, right. Three, there's to be five grand for me to – to do what I want with.' Will had suddenly remembered the conference, where the Nettlefold Award was probably being announced as he spoke. 'Four, there's to be no argument, and I want to go home and my bedroom to be back as it was, by the time I arrive.'

There was a shocked silence. Slowly Noam Throwbones got up and reset the clock, shutting its glass case with precision.

'Will,' said his father, 'you must be sure.'

'There will, in any case, be a review at the age of eighteen,' said the solicitor slowly.

'He's underage, he can't renounce it!' said Mr Shingles shrilly. 'What about my fee?'

'You'll get what you're owed,' said Will's father.

'If he's old enough to inherit, he's old enough to renounce.' Noam Throwbones, Solicitor, cleaned his glasses thoughtfully. 'Nevertheless, it cannot become final until he comes of age—'

'Never mind about all that,' cried Will, making hay with the documents he should have signed, and showering them around the room like confetti. 'Draw up the papers for the Lisle Island Wildlife Trust, and make the directors my mum and dad!'

'But, Will, why? Think of all the things you could have!' His father lifted him off the desk and levelled with him. 'This is a lot of money. It can make us comfortable – can give you everything you want.'

Will hugged him. 'Got everything I want, haven't I? Was Archie happy? Was Jonathan?'

There was another silence, before Mr Shingles packed his briefcase and exited suddenly. 'You'll be hearing from me!'

Then Noam Throwbones ordered in stiff coffees all round, Sprites and sandwiches, and had begun on the rules and conditions for the trust, before Will remembered he had to go.

'Carry on with the rules and stuff. I'm taking a taxi to the Funeral Directors' Conference if you want to know where I am,' he said. 'Might even catch the end of Mantha's speech.'

'Will, wait – where is it?'

'Rendelsham Millennium Hall.'

His mother had watched his face as he turned to go. 'Will, wait—'

'What?'

'It's just – what with the Wildlife Trust, and saving the Pilchard and everything …'

'And?'

'Will, I'm so proud of you.'

'He's more like himself,' he heard her saying as he left the room in a hurry. But that last *proud of you* had rung in his heart all the way to the conference. Now everyone was leaving and he was alone on the steps with Mr Nettlefold. 'I never did know your name,' he said.

'It's Philip. Philip Nettlefold.'

For some reason Will had imagined it would be something exotic. 'Why did I give up the Trice fortune? Well, Phil, because I could see it would twist me. It twisted Archie, even before he had his body stolen. It twisted Hornbeam, when he'd stolen it –'

'Had his *body* stolen?'

'– and it made Jonathan unhappy; he said so himself in his book. Twisted, as in making you do negative things to get more money. I didn't want that to happen to me. I wanted things back the way they were, before any of this happened – can you understand that?'

Phil Nettlefold looked into the eyes of the erstwhile Trice heir and reflected that he was just a young boy with his life in front of him, much as he'd been himself before his father had handed on the business to him, like a stone. 'Yes, I suppose I can.'

'Plus now the island's safe from development,' Will added happily. 'Seals and puffins for ever!'

'Well,' admitted Phil Nettlefold, 'that *is* a good—'

'Nettlefold & Dad – funeral parlour, Rendelsham Road.' Will stepped into a taxi. He emptied Hornbeam's pockets of some soggy notes. 'Have a drink on me. Celebrate the award. I learned a lot. Thanks for everything.'

'You learned a lot? Where?'

'Sure she'll tell you about it. Suppose she's gone home. I'm off to find Mantha,' Will said.

Mantha's Mirror

'I see you're yourself again.'

'Whatever that is.'

'So you gave him his body back – that has to be a first.'

Will's hand was on the cold-room door when something made him hesitate. Mantha had beaten him back to Nettlefold's despite the swift taxi ride through uncluttered streets – but who was she talking to?

'Thanks for the red herring.' A chill ran through Will's heart. *Unmistakably Hornbeam.*

'The Romania story? I only called the *Daily News*; it wasn't rocket science. Why do you look so hideous?'

'Got knocked down, getting away.'

'Again? Thought you'd have learned after Archie.'

'Circulation's failing – I need a new body *now*.'

'Don't look at me for help. You caused enough trouble this time.'

Will applied his eye to the door jamb. He could see the two of them confronting one another, Mantha still removing her gloves and tucking away her papers from the conference.

Hornbeam looked as though he'd been chewed by a very large dog. The end of his collar stuck out. His trousers were ripped, showing his weedy legs. 'They wanted to take me to hospital again,' he whined. 'I only got away by chance.'

'I don't care, do I? A quick call to the paper's all I owe you,' said Mantha, briskly. 'Do what you're going to do, but don't bother me.'

'I could *make* you care – anyone seen your beauty routine lately?'

'Made any elixir for your next jump? Thought not,' Mantha countered. 'You're missing a vital ingredient. That's right – *the boy used it up.*'

Hornbeam's jaw dropped.

'You can check all you want. I've got the last smidgeon. I might even have to destroy it.'

'You – wouldn't.'

She looked at him steadily. 'Try me.'

A croaking laugh. 'Think I might go to Romania.'

'What an amazingly good idea.'

'Let me see the mirror.'

'The mirror's put away.'

Another laugh. 'Staying here, are we?'

'Maybe.'

'Growing mortal, growing old, popping your clogs?'

'If the alternative's ending up like you – then, yes,' said Mantha. 'Being mortal's not so bad. Specially when you're the star of the conference.'

'Dust,' hissed Hornbeam. 'Dust and ashes, and you know it.'

'I don't care, I'm tired,' said Mantha. 'Go or stay, make your mind up.'

'It isn't as easy as that.' Hornbeam grew threatening. 'You can't just dissolve an old partnership at the drop of a hat.'

'Yes, I can.' Mantha dropped a hat from the stand. 'Dissolved. Finis. Now go.'

'It's the boy, isn't it?'

'Will Dudgeon's real, and you're not.'

'Still dust,' hissed Hornbeam, 'and ashes.'

'You're a wraith – a monster – now go!'

'Ashes, and dust – like you.'

Mantha threw a book at him. 'Get out! It's over!'

'For the moment,' murmured the old bodysnatcher, retiring like a wisp of smoke towards the door. Will flattened himself against the wall with seconds to spare before Hornbeam rattled down the steps to the vaults with surprising agility for an old man who'd just been run over.

• ● •

Closing the cold-room door behind him, Will regarded her icily. '*What partnership?*'

'Oh, it's you.' Amaranth Nettlefold took out her gloves again, smoothed down the fingers, folded them neatly. 'Partnership?' she asked lightly.

'I heard everything. Explain.'

'You're Will Dudgeon, in Will Dudgeon's body, isn't that enough?'

'Explain,' Will demanded, putting his body between herself and the door.

'Have you any idea how lucky you are?' She unfolded the gloves, turned them over, folded them again. 'It's never happened before, in the history of – well, in the history of "Hornbeam".' She quoted the name with her fingers.

'Which is?'

'Oh, I think you know.'

'And how do you fit in?'

'Please, Will.' Her eyes met his. 'Please, Will, don't make me show you. I know I owe you an explanation, though it was Hornbeam who swapped—'

'I've been old, I've been crippled, had to get up four times in the night for the loo – haven't I suffered enough?'

'All that'll happen to you anyway, in time,' Mantha said sadly. 'It was *to escape that*, that Hornbeam and I … Come this way.'

Leading him swiftly into a private room behind one of the freezers that he'd never known existed before, she whipped a velvet drape off the Chinese mirror he hadn't even missed from the hall. 'Stand in front of it – what d'you see?'

'Me, of course.' Glorious me! Will flexed a pec and

struck a few poses. How good was it to feel a healthy fart coming on? Better out than in.

'I know you're thirteen, but please.'

Will grinned. He had a talent for ruining the moment, always had.

'Now me.' Mantha stepped in front of the mirror. 'Before you look, remember me as I am now.'

Will took stock. Glorious Mantha! His heart swelled in admiration of her. How truly emo she was, with her unique personal styling, her plea from the heart for green burials …

'I know about the jumping from life to life, but how did sailor Hornbeam get hooked up with you in the undertaking business, anyway?'

'That's another story.'

'How did you first know about Hornbeam, the recipe, what he does? Exactly how long have you known him, and why d'you help him?'

Putting her hand over his mouth, she led him in front of the mirror. 'Look again.'

O horror! There he stood, hale and rosy, holding the hand of a skeleton! Now it had a melting face. Now it was Mantha, now it wasn't. At last the vision settled, and she was old – very old. Hairless, the crown; yellow, the face; staring, the eyes; crippled, the limbs; toothless, the mouth. Yet – yet it was her. The spider 'fascinator', or half-a-felt-hat, clung grotesquely to the side of the skull. The mouth moved – the arms reached out to him.

Will leapt, and the vision had vanished. And there she stood, Mantha as she lived and breathed – as she was, but not as she was, now that he'd seen her reflection.

'I'm as old as the hills, you see,' whispered the perfect lips in the lovely frame. 'There's always a Mantha, always a Hornbeam, down the ages, in many different disguises.'

'I don't understand – is Mr Nettlefold always your dad?'

'Many fathers, many rebirths, many appearances – yet always Mantha in her mirror, growing older and older, unable to escape her fate. Now, look again!'

Will had learned to be wary of the Chinese mirror, but he drew close and peered into the pond of his own mind, and saw that he knew things he didn't know he knew – many things. And here was 'Archie', peering into the same mirror, seeing Lily Lavender, his cousin's love-child, and her daughter, and her daughter – and his, Will's, mother – and himself, dressed as a toothbrush, and on a carnival float!

'He saw you – he chose you – *Hornbeam saw the future …*'

'Me,' Will said. 'In your mirror.'

Mantha nodded. 'That's how he sets up his victims.'

A dark cloud of anger welled up in Will's heart for all those people targeted by 'Hornbeam'. 'What did he originally look like?'

Her voice was faint and fading. 'Don't know – limit of my knowledge – fourteenth-century version …'

The mirror swirled with dark visions, and Will saw a man in medieval clothing treating a ragged child to a rousing tankard of something or other. A dark-haired woman appeared, tore away the tankard and threw its smoking contents on the ground. Not this one, either, she seemed to say …

'I've tried to limit his villainy through the ages.' The being calling itself 'Mantha' sighed. 'It hasn't always been possible. I've become cynical, hard …'

'You're a swapper too?'

'I'm reborn in places of my choosing, entangled with the parasite "Hornbeam" – until now. I may – perhaps finally – be free.' Her eyes shone and she licked her lips. 'The mirror shows what I truly look like. I suffer, as you see. And I *never look into its depths* – which show me my own mind, my own life – and in a way, make it all possible.' She offered him a hammer from the bench. 'I know how you feel … All those victims …'

Will looked grim.

'So smash it, and end my existence.'

Will took the hammer. 'What do you mean?'

'Smash it, and I'm ashes and dust.' Mantha clasped her hands.

The mirror shone before him when all at once a scream so terrible that it set the freezers ringing brought them panting into the frosty air of the cold room.

'It's down in the vaults.'

They looked at one another. Will licked his lips and

strengthened his grip on the hammer. 'Come on then,' he said.

· ● ·

Something was screaming like an animal. A flash of movement in the red-lit darkness. Will rubbed his eyes. 'Come on!'

As Mantha clattered after him down the steps, something twisted and died on a thin scream in the close air.

Will rounded the corner. 'Hornbeam!'

'Your health!' With glittering eyes, Hornbeam raised a last secret phial of elixir. Over his shoulder he wore the large rat he'd just half throttled.

'No! Hornbeam! Don't do it!'

'Can barely … breathe. No … choice. Thanks for the … holiday in your life!'

'We care about you! Wait!'

But the old man had thrown back his head and had fallen down, like a deflated balloon, in the same moment.

Mantha appeared at Will's shoulder. In the next moment the large rat, all at once revived, was sitting on Hornbeam's chest. Its eyes glittered and it stood up on its hind legs, pawing the air in defiance.

'Unbelievable! He's exchanged with a rat!'

'Scat!'

With a last squeak out of the hearing range of most

mortals, the rat scuttled away into the red-lit gloom, its tail switching over the dusty floor and disappearing amongst the caskets.

Will felt mortified beyond anything he would have believed, if someone had told him his life would finally be rid of Hornbeam. But in what a way!

'We should've given him half a chance. I wrote to him. He could've died and had the best funeral ever, as Hornbeam.'

'He chose otherwise. A last phial of elixir – can you believe it? Condemned to the animal realm, he won't be able to make any more. Don't you see? He's trapped!'

Somewhere a rattle and a shriek confirmed that the rat Hornbeam had met with other rats.

'He'll meet problem after problem. He won't be happy. He can't escape what he's done.'

Will nodded, truly sorry for him. Mantha bent compassionately and smoothed the hair of the body. 'Poor sailor.'

'Looks like you've got a funeral to arrange.' Will bowed stiffly, like the old gent he so recently was, and found himself saying, 'I leave you to your strange fate.'

He offered her the hammer, handle first.

She took it; acknowledged him with a nod. 'And I leave you to yours.'

In Perpetuity

The new flower boy was Garry Wilkins from the deprived side of the mainland where no one ever went anywhere, and weekends were spent scamming for money or smoking up the rec.

Now he had a job splaying lilies in a long-necked silver vase on the gleaming desk of the only hotel on Lisle Island, a place which had filled the view from his scabby bedroom ever since he could remember, but which he never imagined he'd visit – until he'd been summoned by Mike.

'Been a lottery,' Mike had announced. 'You're It.'

'It, what?'

'Flower boy, up the hotel. Pays nicely, and it's a doss.'

This had appealed to Garry Wilkins no end, and here he was working his third Saturday in a row without having spilled a single drop of water over the polished floors. Though he got bored easily and had walked off the job and been brought back twice so far, he thought he might stick it this time, at least till the summer, when fishing off the jetty started again.

'Finished reception yet?' Mrs Rhymer swept up in an odd maroon dress splashed with dots, as though someone had tripped up with a tray of measles.

'I'm on it, aren't I?'

'You mean, yes, Mrs Rhymer, I'm just doing it, and I won't be long over the dining-room troughs. And don't just dump those lilies in. And I hope you're bruising the ends.'

Garry Wilkins watched her go and made a face. But he jumped up to help when an old gentleman came in.

'All right on those steps? Take a seat.' He helped the old gent to find a magazine. 'Mandy on reception'll be here in a minute. She's just seeing some people to their room.'

He finished a vase and came back. 'Can I get you a coffee or something?'

'I'm fine, thank you,' said the old gent.

'You look like you need to put your feet up,' Garry said, betraying his kindly nature.

'You're a nice lad. Is the fishing good around here?'

'It is, as it goes. Sometimes we get gar, off the jetty. Slimy, and no good for eating. But bass – sometimes we get bass.'

The old gentleman nodded. 'Well, I'll let you get on.'

'Not in a draught, are you?' Garry closed the main door.

Will thoroughly approved of kindness towards the

elderly. His seat in the cocktail lounge gave him an excellent view of reception and the adjoining bar. A noisy bunch of twitchers had just breakfasted beside him, and he'd pointed out places to go. They'd left armed with flasks and sticks, ablaze with the joy of ticking off another visiting bird on their list. And it wasn't just the grey army – they were attracting kids as well.

Trays along the bar holding leaflets advertising 'Swimming with Seals' already needed refilling. The Lisle Island Wildlife Trust had been up and running for four months already, the website had attracted almost two thousand hits, and the directors, David and Annie Dudgeon, had appointed two Wildlife Wardens – there was even a chance of a feature on local television news!

Parting the ferns beside the fountain, Will gave the old gentleman sitting quietly in reception thumbs-up.

Taking out an envelope from his briefcase, the old gentleman rose. He cleared his throat. 'A-hem!'

'Call Mandy for you, shall I?' Garry put down his buckets.

'I haven't come to stay. I've come to speak to you.'

'I never meant nothing by spraying the flats, I—'

'It isn't about the graffiti. You've nothing to worry about – quite the reverse.'

The old gent extended the envelope. 'Here's five hundred pounds for you.'

Garry looked baffled.

'Five hundred pounds,' repeated the old gent.

'What for?'

The old gentleman smiled kindly. 'I'm a solicitor, name of Throwbones. It's a condition of the job that the flower boy accepts the same amount yearly, in perpetuity.'

'Do what?'

'Ask no questions,' joked Mike, watching the scene.

'You're having a laugh! Why?'

'Probably something they found out.' Mike gestured over his head. 'Don't ask me, ask him.'

Archie – young Archie, before Hornbeam – looked down from his picture over the bar, and as the new flower boy pocketed his cheque with shining eyes and new hope in his heart, Will could have sworn that he winked.